PEN(
THE N   ER

Kamini Patel is a lawyer who dabbles in her family business. After majoring in international relations from Boston University and, later, getting a law degree, she was still at a crossroads as to what she wanted to do with her life. An initial stint as a freelance journalist made her realize that writing is her calling. This resulted in her first novel, *The Morning After*; she hopes to become a full-time writer soon. In her free time Kamini plays a mean game of tennis and indulges in many cooking and baking adventures! Having been raised in five different countries, she is currently settled in Ahmedabad.

THE MORNING AFTER

KAMINI PATEL

Penguin
metro reads

PENGUIN METRO READS

Published by the Penguin Group

Penguin Books India Pvt. Ltd, 11 Community Centre, Panchsheel Park, New Delhi 110 017, India

Penguin Group (USA) Inc., 375 Hudson Street, New York, New York 10014, USA

Penguin Group (Canada), 90 Eglinton Avenue East, Suite 700, Toronto, Ontario, M4P 2Y3, Canada (a division of Pearson Penguin Canada Inc.)

Penguin Books Ltd, 80 Strand, London WC2R 0RL, England

Penguin Ireland, 25 St Stephen's Green, Dublin 2, Ireland (a division of Penguin Books Ltd)

Penguin Group (Australia), 250 Camberwell Road, Camberwell, Victoria 3124, Australia (a division of Pearson Australia Group Pty Ltd)

Penguin Group (NZ), 67 Apollo Drive, Rosedale, Auckland 0632, New Zealand (a division of Pearson New Zealand Ltd)

Penguin Group (South Africa) (Pty) Ltd, 24 Sturdee Avenue, Rosebank, Johannesburg 2196, South Africa

Penguin Books Ltd, Registered Offices: 80 Strand, London WC2R 0RL, England

First published in Penguin Metro Reads by Penguin Books India 2012

Copyright © Kamini Patel 2012

ISBN 9780143417385

Typeset in Adobe Garamond Pro by Eleven Arts, Delhi
Printed at Manipal Technologies Ltd, Manipal

For my parents, may we always laugh through the madness

CONTENTS

BULGE MATTERS

'Why don't you wear your green strapless dress?' asks Sanya. *I should've known.*

'Are you kidding me? That would be like screaming out, forget the coffee, have me instead!'

'Well why not? He sounds like the one to me. Plus, a little bit of action would finally end your dry spell,' scorns Sanya.

Sanya is over to help me pick out an appropriate evening outfit for a coffee 'meeting' with Rajesh. I don't really know why she thinks she would be of any help considering we are total opposites in everything, especially our sense of style. She prefers to walk around in south Mumbai, even while veggie shopping, in micro minis and tank tops, whereas I am almost always dressed in jeans. Her idea of sexy is a skimpy outfit that shows off her long legs, slender neck and back; I am most comfortable when I cover my short and thin frame. Her striking features stand out against her peaches-and-cream complexion; my only prominent feature is my protruding nose. With large cat eyes, further enhanced by kohl, and a perfect pout she knows exactly how to make heads turn anywhere she goes. It doesn't matter what she is wearing, her sexy body language and her 'dare me' attitude catches every man's attention.

a separate words,

'Thanks, but just remember I intend to marry this kid, not use him for a one-night stand. Plus I just can't see myself doing it with him.' I find it hard to say the word 'sex' out loud.

'What?' Sanya is horrified. 'That means he doesn't attract you? Cancel the date right now. Do you have any idea how important sex is in a relationship? Sex is everything!'

'Umm, Sanya, it's a "meeting" and not a date. There's a difference.'

Sanya is too shocked and finds it impossible to believe that sex hasn't come into the picture yet! I don't know, I'm just not there yet. He seems . . . I don't know.

Sanya disrupts my train of thought, 'Ahem, are you dreaming of him naked?' I presume the disgusted look on my face gives her the answer. Frustrated, she asks, 'Have you at least kissed him?'

'Nope.'

'Well, then, you better kiss him tonight. Did you get a look at his bulge? Remember what they say, if it's big, it's either his penis or his wallet, and either way you win!' she laughs.

'Oh shut up, Sanya. Now what do you think of this shirt?' I hold up a white top.

'No,' she brushes off my choice.

Exasperated I ask her, 'So, what are you doing tonight? How come you don't have any plans?'

'I'm staying in. Sanjay said he would call tonight to discuss the developments for the new fund since he has time.'

Now what does that mean?

'So, you are waiting for him to call you?' Sanya never waits. And she never spends an evening at home on her own.

Sanya's face flushes, 'Well, no, that's not the reason why I'm staying in. I'm just spending time home for a change!'

'Oh, right, that makes sense,' I raise an eyebrow. Sanya just never does that—stay at home, and do nothing. 'Just be careful, Sanya, he is married, remember? Don't get too carried away.'

'I will not. I'll be fine,' she says a bit too strongly. 'Okay, I think I've found the top for you!'

Sanya worries me. She always says the wrong things at the wrong time, falls in love with the wrong kinds, and almost always manages to get past it one way or another. Among my three best friends, Sanya Mukherjee is the troublemaker. She is a social worker but in the page three style. She loves her expensive toys and accessories and has never really worked a day in her whole life. She is carefree, wild and impulsive, the kind who gets a kick out of sticking up her middle finger at a passing school bus. Every month brings a new man into her kitty, one that she might pick up from absolutely anywhere! Sanya is capable of going out to buy toothpaste and returning with a hot date. But for now, she is unbelievably smitten by Sanjay Jhunjhunwala, a married man, whom she met at a social do recently and who has promised to give a very big donation to her charity initiative for slum children. She is conveniently forgetful of the fact that Mr Jhunjhunwala has a wife, and we pray that this, too, shall pass as just another fling on her long list!

'What are Palak and Lara up to?' I ask, referring to our two best friends.

'I have no idea, maybe I'll call them, see if they wanna grab some coffee.'

'Coffee?' I ask unbelievingly. The four of us aren't really known for being coffee addicts; the poison that binds us is alcohol.

Palak Mehta and I have known each other since childhood. Both of us passed out of universities in London, she with a finance degree, and I a communications degree. Palak at twenty-six, is tall, intelligent and incredibly attractive: strong jaw line, big eyes and a beautiful smile. And her charm lies in the fact that she is absolutely unaware of her beauty—always tying up her luscious locks in a professional ponytail that only enhances her bone structure and her beautiful eyes are forever hidden behind rimless glasses. She is fast moving up the corporate ladder at a multinational consulting firm. Palak is the one who I go to for advice, who kicks sense into me and grounds me to earth! She has been in a steady relationship with Raj Choudhary since college.

Lara Sen is a fashion designer who specializes in elegant evening dresses and caters to almost every socialite and celebrity in Mumbai. Her regular clientele boasts of the most beautiful and famous women of the country. She possesses an elegant, traditional and simple taste which reflects in her designs. Lara is a classic Bengali beauty with long hair, cute dimples and the most delicate pair of hands ever. She is engaged to Ashish Agrawal, whom she met three years ago. She is currently busy battling her future in-laws. Lara is at constant loggerheads with Ashish's parents and sisters, but regardless of how many tearful nights they give her, she remains firmly in love with Ashish.

Sanya laughs, 'Yeah, what am I saying? A bar it is!'

After much convincing on both sides, I am ready with light blue skinny jeans and a summery yellow blouse with ruffles in the front. Teamed with my white heels and a matching white tote I am ready for an evening coffee date. NO! An evening coffee *meeting*. I refuse to refer to arranged setups as dates. Even if this is the sixth one . . . with the same guy.

Rajesh messages: 'Come downstairs in 2.'

He's a stickler for punctuality. Butterflies in my stomach do a somersault, an odd occurrence, since I usually don't experience such emotions.

This guy must be something to have this effect on me! Ugh, I hate being so nervous.

I check myself again before getting into the elevator with Sanya and my neighbour, an elderly man we address as Dadaji. Sanya purposely fumbles, pretending to help me with the blouse buttons by my breasts to make poor old Dadaji squirm while she grins mischievously.

'Sanya, stop it!' I urgently whisper, trying to push her away.

When Sanya steps out on the third floor for her apartment, she cheekily turns around and shouts, 'Don't forget, check out his bulge!'

The elevator door shuts with her smiling widely and pointing vulgarly at her crotch.

Oh shit, she did not just do that!

I am the colour of a red traffic light as I timidly turn to look at Dadaji, praying he didn't understand. But judging by his disapproving face, he definitely did! An indication to the crotch means the same thing in every generation!

Just as I walk out of the lift, still recoiling from the embarrassment, Rajesh pulls up in his fancy Mercedes. My luck is always just great!

When I slide into the car, he takes my hand and says, 'You look beautiful.'

From the colour of beetroot, I think I'm turning into a new shade of crimson. Every word he utters sounds and feels different. A flirty comment seems so genuine from him. I am usually only flattered by aunties and my girlfriends, who say good things mostly to boost my self-esteem or to distract the attention away from my protruding nose.

Cloud nine sure feels good.

Rajesh asks, 'Instead of coffee, want to go for a drink? And then we can take it from there?'

He sounds hopeful and the thought of a cool screwdriver lights up my face.

'Sure, I think that's a better idea. Let's go to Amadeus?'

Driving towards Marine Drive, I realize that a vodka drink at 6.30 p.m. would not portray me in such good light. But I need something hard, not wine, to get through this meeting with him.

Maybe a cosmopolitan will do. What drink will he choose? He seems like a single malt guy.

In my booze-infested world, much of a guy's personality can be determined by his choice of drink. In short, it indicates whether your man is indeed a man, or not. We reach Amadeus in comfortable silence; I'm too nervous to talk and he seems preoccupied. As we get out of the car I discreetly glance at his attire; he is wearing fitted jeans and a loose white shirt, presumably an attempt to broaden his small build but with little success.

He walks over and places his hand at the small of my back. He smiles as his large eyes glint with mischief.

Why am I squirming? And does he need to touch me in public?

'So, what will you have?' he asks as we settle down at the bar.

'Umm . . .' trying my best not to blurt out vodka, 'I'll have a cosmopolitan.'

He calls the bartender and orders, 'Two cosmos please!'

What? What did he just say? Are you kidding me? Did he just order a 'Sex and the City' drink for himself? Oh my God! My gaydar turns on to pick up on possible signals. *Maybe that's why I can't imagine kissing him; let alone having sex!*

Rajesh turns to me and feels the fabric of my top and says, 'This colour really suits you, you should wear bright colours all the time.'

Gay! Gay! Gay!

Giving a weak smile, I try to change the topic to less feminine ones, 'Thanks. So how was your day?'

'It was good. Just relaxed, watched a movie. How was yours?'

Hmm, he sounds lazy. And gay.

'Good, I finished off a lot of small errands that were pending for a while. I met Sanya for a bit.'

Our girly cosmos arrive and my nausea returns.

Why on earth would a guy order a cosmopolitan?

We pick up our drinks, clink and sip. Well, he sips, I gulp.

Maybe a macchiato would have been a better option after all. My knight in shining armour drinks cosmopolitans! Jesus Christ!

Since I cannot restrain myself any more, I purse my lips before I cautiously ask, 'So, what do you normally drink?'

'Mostly whisky or beer. And I absolutely love wine. I can't wait to go on a wine-tasting trip.' He narrows his eyes and adds, 'Especially with you.'

I blush more out of anger than shyness: *Why the hell is he drinking a cosmo right now then?*

My phone beeps and it's a message from Sanya: 'Did you check out his bulge? How big is it?'

I try with all my might to not look down at his crotch.

Neha, get a grip, he just ordered a cosmo, most likely there is no bulge. And why am I still nervous and jittery as hell? This is the sixth time we are meeting. Can this mean that I might actually like him? I, Neha Shah, will be marrying a cosmo-drinker? Really?

I glance over and see his large toad-like eyes and wonder what it is about this frog that is making me want to see him again and again. Our first drinks finish, mine faster than his, while he talks non-stop about his passion for wines.

The bartender returns to ask if we want a second round and Rajesh looks over enquiringly, 'Want to have another one and then eat dinner here? Or do you have to go somewhere?'

Common sense tells me to say no to dinner with a cosmo-drinker, but I hear myself saying, 'Sure, we can have dinner.'

Crap, why can't I control my tongue. Okay, now just go with the flow and see where the night ends up. But, does this mean that he likes me? Is he interested? Ugh, Neha, stop with the questions, you never understood the male psyche, so don't bother trying now.

'You want the same? Or go for wine?'

'Wine,' I blurt out a bit too fast. The horrors of having another cosmo with him would be unbearable. 'I don't mind either red or white—you pick.'

'Okay, I'm feeling white. Which one do you recommend tonight?'

The waiter arrives with four bottles and Rajesh takes a good amount of time to read through each bottle's label and then asks to taste each one. I hate it when people do that. I personally believe it's just a way for the pompous to show off. Just pick any damn one, because quite frankly, after one and a half glasses, it all tastes the same. He finally picks one, after swirling, twirling, sipping and nodding his approval.

I could have delivered a baby by now.

'So, which are your favourite whites?' he asks.

Answering this question to an obvious wine-lover is tricky. I choose to be honest and say, 'You caught me, I'm no connoisseur! I can't really tell my Chardonnay from Riesling.'

'Well, I must confess, I consider myself almost an oenologist,' he smiles proudly. He continues, 'But let's talk about you. I've been meaning to ask you about your past relationships. You just mentioned them fleetingly, but I want to know what happened.'

Oh God, the past.

'Well, there isn't much to it. I dated a few guys—one was fairly serious but it didn't work out. We were on paths which weren't crossing. What else do you want to know?'

I detest talking about the past because it has nothing to do with the present or the future. Okay, it does have a lot to do with the present and future, but I really don't want to be admitting how I generally screw up most of my relationships and my incapability when it comes to getting into a committed relationship.

'Well, I want to know if you are over them. And what were the reasons?' he asks pointedly. And the eyes pop out while he sniffs his wine goblet.

'Of course I am, I mean, I wouldn't be here if I wasn't!' I laugh. 'I hardly remember any of them frankly! It all happened a long time ago when I was very young and naïve.'

Does he really expect me to admit that I still occasionally stalk all my exes, flings and crushes? Is he always going to grill me like this? My turn now.

However, I have a more sophisticated way of asking questions.

'And what about you? How many girls' hearts have you broken so far?' I tease. His face reddens slightly and I try to suppress a laugh. 'Stop blushing and tell me the truth!'

'Well, I've had a couple of steady girlfriends before, obviously not all at once!' He adds, 'And I dated a few girls here and there, but nothing materialized into anything too serious. And since the last year I have been seeing girls for marriage set up by my parents or someone or another!'

'Ah, so we have a player here!'

He laughs, his eyes crinkling up cutely, 'No, not at all. I am not the player type. I always look for something substantial. I'm emotional and sensitive, so I can't do that. And I hate breaking up.'

Wow! A man with a heart! Okay, a frog with a heart! Is this a movie? Or maybe it's the wine's effect. He definitely is adorable. He isn't my type, but there is something about him that's keeping me hooked. Or maybe his eagerness to commit is making him attractive.

The waiter appears and tells us that our table is ready. An evening coffee ends up being a dinner date. I think it's safe to say we are passed the 'meeting' stage. We order our dishes; I don't even know what I'm eating, but it all tastes good. And I'm relishing the wine, whatever it is. Post-dessert, I am buzzing, smiling and laughing. A good sign! I have forgivingly forgotten the cosmo incident for the time being. While driving back we hold hands and I realize I haven't been this excited in a very long time.

What's going to happen now? What is he thinking?

Holding hands is usually a good sign, but then again you never know. Experience has taught me nothing actually. I figured it is best to shut my brain when it comes to boys, because they rarely make sense. But this one seems like a thinking man, a rare species!

He drives into the parking spot of my building and turns to me, 'You've been quiet! What are you thinking?'

'Umm . . . nothing, just tired,' I lie. I am a wee bit too drunk, ridiculously nervous and I am sure he has figured it out already.

'Come, I'll take you upstairs. You've had a bit too much to drink,' he says as he gets out of the car.

Great. What have you done now, Neha! He thinks you're an alcoholic. Well, at least he knows the truth!

We keep a safe distance in front of the security guards of my building. As soon as the elevator doors shut, he steps closer to me. I look down, afraid to meet his eyes.

Rajesh softly whispers, 'Don't be so shy, come here beautiful.'

He slides an arm around my waist and cups my face with his other hand, gently forcing my eyes to meet his and murmurs, 'Relax. Do you know how beautiful you are?' He kisses my cheek, just as the elevator doors open.

I gasp in fear of being seen and step back and fumble with my purse, unsure of what to do next. Rajesh smiles adoringly at me, evidently brimming with hope to get a little kiss, perhaps on the lips this time. My hand dives further into my purse searching for my house key. He takes the key from my hand and helps me out of the lift as I struggle with my four-inch heels.

Damn it, Neha, did you have to get so carried away with the wine?

'Neha,' he murmurs softly as he turns to hug me outside my apartment door.

I lose my balance and tumble towards him in a drunken stupor; with his fingers he caresses my hair as he looks into my eyes and comes closer.

Should I kiss him? Or should I not? Damn it, I wish I was sober enough to make wise decisions.

He leans further in and I tremble with hazy confusion, my knees giving away, and I surrender to the stupid side of my brain which instructs me to close my eyes. Then images and thoughts merge into a blur.

WOMEN AND ELEPHANTS NEVER FORGET INJURY

The shrill alarm awakens me from my drunken slumber. As I stretch out to hit the snooze button, a throbbing pain shoots through my head.

What the hell happened?

I struggle in vain to recollect last night's happenings.

The last thing I remember is standing outside my apartment, his lips pressing on mine. *Oh my God, I kissed him! Shit! Why did I let him kiss me, damn it, why did I kiss back? Shit, I don't even remember exactly how our first kiss happened. Ugh, and it's Monday. I hate Mondays, especially when I have a giant hangover.*

I do the only thing that can keep me sane at this hour—call Palak. Lara and Sanya don't do mornings.

'What's wrong?' Palak answers immediately. She knows morning calls can only mean an emergency.

'I got drunk, we kissed, and I don't remember our first kiss. How bad can this be? I don't remember getting into the house. All I remember is we were outside my flat and there was some caressing and a lot of kissing. Palak, he thinks I'm a slut, doesn't he?'

'Shut up, Neha, he doesn't. Plus, I think you quite like him, so you did nothing wrong. Go eat something, feel better and don't you dare call or text him. Let him do it.' Palak is a stickler for chivalry and is a walking dating-etiquette-and-rule book!

'I don't think he will, he ordered a cosmo with me last night; he is one of us Palak,' I freak out over the phone. 'What have I done? I kissed a cosmo-drinking man!'

'Calm down and stop overreacting. How was the kiss? Was it nice?' she giggles.

'I don't bloody remember, Palak! What the hell am I supposed to do?'

'Oh darling, he isn't gay, don't worry. Now go to work, and call me at lunch. Relax and just wait for him to contact you first. Remember it's Monday today, and he is probably late for work too, just like you are!' I look at the time and it's already 8.40 a.m..

Shit, I'm late again.

'Oh God, and I have a meeting with Monica the bitch today.'

'Good luck. And relax Neha, you did not do anything stupid,' she hangs up, laughing pleasantly.

Glad to have been your morning dose of entertainment.

I reach work late, blaming it on the traffic and settle down in my minuscule cubicle with an aspirin and coffee. Not that anyone really cares. I work at a prestigious public relations and event management firm but have a not-so-prestigious lowly position by the file cabinets. It's where I have been since the last three years, when I was forced by my dad to take this job. The words ambition and hard work don't exist in my vocabulary.

The joys of today will be a privileged morning meeting with Monica the bitch, trophy wife to Harry darling, our biggest client. Monica rarely makes it to the a.m. meetings. I assume her mornings usually start six hours after the start of my day.

Harry (originally Harjeet) Chaddha is a sixty plus, rich American NRI return who has grown famous for throwing the most profligate bashes in town for his company, Harry Constructions Limited. The company somehow continues to stay afloat despite the ailing economy, which leads most of us at work to believe he earns the big bucks by smuggling cocaine from Colombia. He is also one of the most annoying clients we have, constantly comparing us to his team in sunny California in his fake American accent. But my boss, Rita, is in love with him and unabashedly flirts with him, addressing him as Harry darling!

His thirty years younger wife, Monica, has apparently graduated with a magna cum laude honours degree from an Ivy League, but obviously lost it somewhere down the line when she visited her plastic surgeon; double D silicones and Botoxed face! One rarely ever sees a reaction from her, but she has mastered the art of voice simulation and projection. Monica fits in perfectly with the stereotypical gold-digging pin-up wife—the curvaceous body, the perfectly groomed face, bouffant hair, long, French manicured nails and permanent make-up. She is rude, obnoxious, insensitive and always inappropriately dressed. Her casual trademark look is a super tight wraparound dress with five-inch heels she wears for any place and time. The excited peons tend to make extra trips into the conference room whenever she is around to ogle at her bulging breasts and bare legs. The inside joke on her is that she is permanently pissed off because her sixty-something husband can't give her any action in bed, making her super frustrated. There are even lewder insinuations that I'd rather not say aloud!

The only advantage of having her on board is that she adds a bit of glamour to an otherwise boring client industry—real estate. And using her in publicity campaigns attracts good, if somewhat perverted, attention.

My colleague Tanya announces, 'The bitch is here.'

When Tanya and I walk into the conference room, Monica is sitting with a bunch of files on the side while delicately shifting through papers with her long, white-tipped talons. Once again she is in her standard morning attire: a teal blue tight wraparound dress, dangerously threatening to tear, oversized black Chanel sunglasses and brown lipstick. A revolting stench of Chanel and cigarettes emanates from her.

Good morning to you, Neha!

'Good morning, Monica,' I fake smile to which she simply frowns, slightly nods and carries on shifting papers (note: not reading).

Rita walks in with a stack of newspapers and smiles cheerfully, 'Good morning, Monica. Saturday's event was a big hit. It was covered in all the major newspapers and here's a gorgeous picture of you!'

Rita is a middle-aged, hardworking single woman, who has set up this prestigious and well-reputed firm from scratch, competing ferociously with the multinationals that have recently infested the territory! She becomes a raging tyrant before any deadline and shares a 'just-hate' relationship with each employee. But her bonus policy and the exposure the company offers are great, so everyone sticks around. And I have nowhere else to go.

A bored Monica perks up at the mention of her photograph. The narcissistic bitch is interested only on topics related to herself. Monica's many moods swing from the North to South Pole, varying upon subject, time of day and the people around. She can be laughing loudly at one minute over a dumb joke and yelling at her secretary the next. Her energy levels peak at various odd moments, which we assume has something to do with the smuggled white powder!

She pours through every paper and smiles satisfyingly at her pictures showing off her brand-new cleavage. Without being asked she orders, 'I'll have a cappuccino with Sugar Free.'

How about a please or a thank you? Bitch.

I willingly offer to fetch her coffee from Barista, leaving Tanya to treasure the joys of taking notes for the next strategy for Harry Construction's new project: service apartments. The problem with this ambitious but doable project (with all that cocaine smuggled dough!) is that the media had recently given bad coverage over land ownership issues and illegal constructions. In public relations, one assumes any publicity is good publicity. But Harry darling tends to take this concept a little too literally, revelling in negative limelight.

I order a coffee for myself as well. People usually hate doing the coffee round, but I love the task: when else can I evade work and get myself a cup of good coffee in the bargain? As I watch the barista froth milk, my mind wanders to last night.

How the hell did that happen? Neha, why did you kiss him? Oh God, what am I to do now? And why has he not called me yet? Or at least texted?

Beep: A BBM.

Finally! This better be Rajesh. Please be Rajesh. Please, please. Shit.

It's Sanya. 'Heard you finally reached second base last night! Did you feel his bulge? Hahaha.'

Girlfriends sure are angels sent from heaven.

Ⴤ

It's already 1 p.m. and Rajesh has not texted or called.

I bet he thinks I am a slut who kisses anyone who drops her home when she gets drunk.

I plop down on my desk, feeling too sick to eat anything. My small cubicle suffocates me further and the office clatter is not helping my pounding head. I try to distract myself by browsing through my emails. There it is, lying in my inbox since 10.45 a.m.: A Facebook friend request from Rajesh Parikh, followed by an email with the subject line: 'I miss you already'. A wave of relief washes over me.

I open it nervously, my stomach churning in anticipation.

```
Dearest Neha,
    Hi beautiful! I thought it would be better
if I didn't disturb your beauty sleep this
morning especially after you politely informed
me how much you hate mornings in general and
Mondays in particular, but I want you to know
that I had an amazing time last night and you
looked absolutely gorgeous; you took my heart
away. I hope that we can continue to get to
know each other better. I hope you turn out
to be everything that I had imagined. Call me
when you get done with work, I've taken the
day off. Mwah!
                                        Rajesh
```

I sit there stunned as my heart does cartwheels. I am definitely touched. An email like this is a first. He is so attentive, sensitive and caring.

Wow, such sorts do exist!

I reread the email a couple of times until my eyes settle on the sentence.

What does he mean by 'I hope you turn out to be everything I had imagined'? What does he really mean by that? Does he have a set of regulations that the girl should adhere by? Is love for excessive alcohol a prerequisite by any chance? Oh whatever! He didn't call or text, but he emailed and that's all I need!

I reach for the phone to call Palak.

'Palak, Rajesh emailed me.'

'He *what*? He dumped you over the internet? Oh I am so sorry my darling, at least thank God he didn't do it over Facebook!' she cackles hideously into the phone.

'Shut up, no, he sent me a friend request AND emailed me to say that he had a great time. I am forwarding you the email. Tell me what you think.'

'Okay, love. Bye.'

She calls back within two minutes, 'I don't know what to make of this. It's such a sweet email, but why did he add that last line, "Hope you turn out to be everything that I had imagined"? Who does he think he is to say that? Neha, you better not change to fit in with him. I think this is a warning sign. I mean who says something like that?'

'I'm not going to change, Palak. But it's such a sweet email; no one has ever done such a thing for me. And he didn't even mention my nose once.'

'Oh please, Neha, there is nothing wrong with your nose. And he isn't exactly Brad Pitt, is he, that he has a right to mention appearances.'

'How do you know?' I ask suspiciously.

'You think I haven't already Facebook stalked him?' laughs Palak. 'By the way, he did in fact date Natasha for a bit.' Natasha is one of the most eligible bachelorettes in the Gujarati society. I listen on. 'And no one knows what happened, so I don't know if it was an arranged set-up or they met on their own. But you know Natasha, if he said something like this to her, she would have definitely ripped him apart!'

'Oh, of course, not everyone is as docile as me,' I groan.

Why am I so tolerant? No. I'm not going to let this prick of a guy get the better of me!

'Neha, you need to know where you stand. Don't get sucked into anything you aren't comfortable with. I'll deal with your mother if you want me to,' Palak says sternly.

'Yes, okay.'

After hanging up I think about last night. I play our entire conversation in my head to try and pick out any other subtle comments he had made that could hint at a rigid guy who would be difficult to handle. But there is no point. I had been too engrossed obsessing about the cosmopolitan incident to remember anything.

'Rita madam *bula rahi hai*,' announces Narayan, the office boy.

Shit! What did I do now?

I fix my hair and knock on her cabin door.

'Come in,' she bellows.

I cautiously enter Rita's impressive cabin. The cream-coloured walls are adorned with various art pieces by famous artists. A Chesterfield sofa set where she enjoys her cup of tea while watching the daily news on her fancy flat screen occupies a corner of the room. It's also used during those times Harry darling pays her a solitary visit! Her cabin spells out opulence in a very tasteful manner. She is an elegant woman no doubt, always dressed in formals with an ornate piece of jewellery and hair tied back or blow-dried. She exudes intelligence, elegance and charisma.

I find Rita sitting straight, working on her computer with reading glasses perched on her nose and her expensive white shirt folded around the wrists. Rita raises her gaze above the spectacles to observe me carefully. Avoiding eye contact, my vision fixates on her chunky red-stoned necklace standing out

vividly against her linen shirt. Her hair is tied back without a
single tendril falling out of place.

'Umm . . . you wanted to see me?'

'Hmm . . . sit,' she motions to the chair in front of her
grand and glossy oak table. She swivels her large leather chair
sideways and scuffles through papers. I struggle to sit upright
trying, in vain, to ignore the pounding in my head.

'Neha,' she starts, placing a thin plastic file in front of her.
I take a deep breath in anticipation. 'You've been here for
almost three years now.' I nod. 'But you've still been in the
same position as a trainee-cum-copywriter.' She scrutinizes
me for a reaction.

I still can't figure out where this is going.

'Do you have any future plans in mind? Do you want to
move up the ladder? Make a career change? Or . . .' she looks
at me expectantly.

'Umm . . .' *I have no idea!* 'I am not so sure,' I mutter.

'Well, you've been here three years, do you like what
you do?'

It's passable.

'Uh, yeah, I do.'

'Would you like to do more?'

NO! 'Uh, yeah, sure.'

Rita stares at me quietly for a long minute, forcing me to
shift uncomfortably on the chair.

'I am opening up two new job posts; both are for assistant
positions to the account executive for Harry's account. I suggest
you consider applying for them. In the next two months I will
be monitoring every worthy candidate closely. Applications
will be out soon. I'd rather promote someone internally
than recruit externally.' She pauses. 'But, you need to prove
yourself.'

I remain silent.

'Think about it. You may go now.'

'Thank you,' I quickly get up and exit.

A promotion? And me? That must be the joke of the century!

🍸

On my way home from work I call Lara.

'Hi,' she greets me in a distracted tone. 'How was it last night? Palak updated me a bit.'

'It was good. But I got drunk. I don't know how and the kissing bit is all too blurry. And he sent me an email today.'

'Yeah, Palak told me. I don't like that he sent you that email. Nor do I like the fact that he just randomly took the day off.'

Lara is a workaholic and despises lazy people, a reason why she is always at loggerheads with a relatively idle Sanya and me.

'I really don't know what to think about it. I'm confused.'

'How do you feel about kissing him?'

'Honestly, I don't know. I feel numb.'

'Numb? Neha? You feel numb?' she asks, bewildered. 'Don't you feel excited? Or all blushy and giggly?' Lara is a real romantic.

'No, well, I do, but you know, I'm not so sure.'

'Neha, just relax. Give it some time. Have you called him yet?'

'No. I don't want to talk to him right now. I'm trying to get over the fact that we kissed so soon.'

'Shut up; it isn't so soon. Plus, he does like you, that's clear. Now it's a question of whether you like him or not.'

'Hmm . . .' I bury my face in my hand, my head is still pounding. 'How's everything with you?'

'Oh my God, don't ask,' Lara starts out. 'Ashish's mother is driving me nuts. They want to throw a bloody engagement party now, four months after we have been engaged! Like seriously, how dumb is that? The party should have been ages ago! Besides I just want to focus on the wedding now instead of getting distracted by an engagement party.'

Ashish's family never accepted Lara when they were dating and when Ashish put his foot down and brought Lara home, it wasn't exactly the most ecstatic moment in their house. Hence, there wasn't a big bash or any kind of public celebration. Each day proves to be a battle for Lara; the mother refuses to speak directly with her, preferring to pass messages and snide comments through her younger daughters, Divya and Riya, who are also not particularly fond of Lara.

'I am honestly trying with every bit of my energy to get along with her and the rest of the family, and to keep things as peaceful as I can. But she makes it impossible for me to do that, especially when she won't talk to me!' She sounds frustrated and on the verge of tears. 'Now we are quarrelling over the guest list. She has over a thousand people, whereas I have cut mine down to 400, including family and friends. But she refuses to shorten her list. I wanted a destination wedding so we don't have to bother with all this, but she just doesn't want to hear about it.'

'And Ashish? What does he want?'

'Ashish is staying out of it,' she exhales dejectedly. 'He says that I should figure it out with his mother and he only wants the wedding to be a lot of fun with a lot of booze.'

I laugh, 'Yes, please, an open bar!'

'Yeah, but let's get to the wedding first! I just wish Ashish would be more supportive, especially since I will have to live with them.'

'Oh man! Dude, how are you going to live with them?'

'I know. I'm so dreading it. But I intend to be in my studio all day long, so that we both can be at peace.'

'Escapism is the best route.'

'No, it's not. I don't like it. But I have no other choice. Each olive branch I pass on gets thrown on the ground and stomped upon. There is less than a year left for the wedding and we really should start sorting out our differences.' She takes a deep breath. 'Last time when I offered to make her outfits for the wedding, I got to know through Divya that she had said, "I hate Lara's taste." I am so mad! How dare she insult my work!' I cannot help laughing. 'I'm serious! I wanted to punch her in the face. But then I think of Ashish and cool down.'

'Her taste is really bad isn't it?'

She snorts, 'Oh my God, yes! It is so horrible. Her style has typical nouveau-riche written all over it, all blingy and gaudy. This is why I want to make her outfit; to prevent her from looking hideous at my wedding!'

I laugh on. 'That's a good idea,' I agree.

'I'm really glad Ashish's style is not influenced by them. I have offered to design stuff for the rest of his family. Hopefully I can make them look sober and decent! Oh shit, Divya is calling again; I'll speak to you later. Bye! Oh, and you should speak to Rajesh today. Okay?'

'Okay, bye!'

She's right, but what shall I say? So umm hey, are you a great kisser because I don't remember much?

Oh shit, I forgot to tell Lara about my meeting with Rita. Oh well, who cares, it's not like I am going to bother with it.

CASTLES MADE OF SAND

'So, how do you like this Rajesh kid, Neha?' Dad asks while reading the evening papers, one of the few moments he relishes in peace from the hectic life of running an export business.

My mother is busy painting her perfectly manicured nails pearl pink while she waits for her puke-green face mask to dry. Appearances are everything for my mother. But I have to admit she looks stunning for her age. A vigorous exercise schedule, a strict beauty regime and an occasional Botox session helps her maintain herself for her rather hectic social life. I am the complete opposite, much to her disappointment.

I hesitantly reply, 'I don't know yet, Dad, it's only been a few weeks!'

'It's been a month already, Neha!' blurts out my mother.

I roll my eyes in protest. 'Well, I think . . . I *think* he seems a bit too romantic,' I make a face.

Dad stoically replies, 'Sorry my love, but they just don't make men like they used to any more!'

My socialite mother cuts in, 'Doesn't he look a little bit like . . . a . . . a . . .' struggling to speak with the mud mask on she finds the appropriate word, 'A frog!'

I can't help but laugh at how correctly she described him! He does in fact look quite like a frog. But a cute one!

'But, Neha, please, do think about it carefully and try not to keep changing your mind!' she says sternly.

I have a fairly restless and indecisive soul, which makes it rather difficult for me to make quick decisions, and is probably the reason why I am still single! And since I haven't been very successful at the boyfriend hunt, my mother has taken it upon herself to ensure that her only daughter gets married very soon. My mother's constant nagging and hyperventilating drives me up the wall almost every day. Aunties make it worse by fuelling my mother's tensions. Moreover, they insist upon giving plenty of free advice on how to know who the right one to marry is, particularly about the 'spark'. She fretted, preached and annoyed the crap out of me until I relented to meet Rajesh. An arranged marriage is not going to be an easy feat for me or my parents!

At the age of twenty-five, I am wiser to the ways of the world than I was a few years ago, and have cut down the 'tall, dark and handsome' criteria, to a mere 'should be taller than me'. But I still insist on a good education (should have a degree and a job!), basic manners and social skills. I'm not reaching for the stars, just for someone, who can stand on his own two feet, has a good heart, who is smart, funny, huggable and lovable. Am I asking for too much? Apparently so, because none of these qualities seem to exist in one man if we are to go by my groom-hunt so far.

'I gotta feeling . . . Tonight's gonna be a good night . . .' my BlackBerry rings.

It's Rajesh.

Shit.

I haven't spoken to him since the fateful night, which was two nights ago.

'Hey . . . umm . . . where've you been?'

'Sorry, I've just been running around. I'm late for a work event now, so I gotta rush. I'll call you later?'

'Uh, okay. Did you get my email?'

'Yeah . . . Uh . . . Thanks, that was really nice.'

'Are we good?'

'Yes, yes, Rajesh, we're good,' I smile in spite of myself. 'I'll call you after.'

'Okay, bye.'

A weird feeling churns in my gut. I had almost forgotten this wonderful feeling of anxiety and excitement. Despite being so confused, I welcome the feeling.

My phone rings again.

Palak greets, 'Hi Neha, how you doing?'

'Blah, but Rajesh called.'

'What? Ooh, what did he say?'

'He asked if I'd got his email. I said yes and then I hung up.'

'Wow, Neha, you really can't deal with anything uncomfortable can you?' Palak laughs.

'Hmm, I'm on my way to the Oberoi. I have a work event tonight.'

'Oh, I forgot to tell you that night when you were with Rajesh, we all went to 212,' Palak updates me.

'Did Sanya come? She told me she was *waiting* for Sanjay to call her,' I ask.

'Yeah, she came for a bit but left surprisingly early.'

'So did you guys have fun?' I ask.

'Yes, and guess what? Ashish whispered to me when Lara wasn't looking that his family has agreed to get a separate place for them after marriage. But he wants to be sure before he tells Lara, so keep your mouth shut.'

'Wow! That's awesome! I am so glad,' I exclaim.

Knowing how Ashish's mother is such a terror, only if I loved a guy as much as Lara loved Ashish would I put up with the treatment the mother-in-law gives her. And considering how important the joint family tradition is for Ashish's conservative parents, letting them get their separate place comes as a welcome surprise.

'Oh and Sanya got hit on by a woman!' Palak adds.

'What?'

Sanya attracts lustful attention everywhere; her full lips, flawless complexion, feline eyes, thick wavy brown hair and a sexy hourglass figure does not even escape the female gaze it seems.

Palak laughs, 'Yeah, she was quite elated. She has decided that if she isn't married within two years she will change her preferences. She believes she has it in her to enter the new league! Don't be shocked if she turns up at the next gay parade!'

'Oh my God, why am I not surprised? Oh wait, Sanya is calling; I'm putting you on conference.'

'Hi babes,' sings Sanya. 'Palak did you update the exciting news to Neha? Neha, I'm going to become a lesbian in two years if I don't get hitched by then. I got hit on by a gorgeous girl last night and I think it's not a bad way of life,' Sanya proudly states. Palak and I are still in splits. 'Oh and Ishaan, Vick and Abhi were there too, and Ishaan was with a super hot but bitchy model once again.'

The three guys are close friends of Raj and Ashish. Ishaan, a serial model dater, is the most promiscuous of the lot, always surrounded by a number of girls and he always manages to make a party rock. He is a handsome man, standing tall at 6 feet, broad built, gets cute dimples when he smiles and has a charismatic personality. Vick and Abhi are the jokers, the ones who entertain the rest of us while Ishaan is busy with his six-feet tall, skinny, super hot and super ditzy date for the night!

'By the way, Sanya, where did you go last night?' Palak asks casually.

'Huh? I was with you guys,' Sanya's voice goes up a pitch.

'No. I mean after. You disappeared! Vick said he saw you on the phone and then you got into someone's car?'

'What? No way. Vick was probably drunk and mistook someone else for me,' she answers uneasily.

'Oh okay,' responds Palak.

I remain quiet. Sanya is up to something that she is not telling us. Does it involve Mr Married?

'Anyways, dah-lings!' Sanya brightens up, trying to change the topic. 'Can we go for a champagne brunch some time soon? It's been ages since our last one,' she asks.

Uh oh! Our brunch usually lasts over four hours and ends with us stumbling out of the restaurant totally sloshed. None of us ever remember how we get home!

'Oh yes, perfecto! I'm in. We haven't blacked out together in a while!' comments Palak.

Four drunk girls can only mean extreme drama and intense revelations. But then, what's life without a little drama?

⚲

Perfect boys exist on paper. Then why does the perfection distort when they come alive in person. Rajesh would be an excellent example. But aren't I also distorted in real? Okay, yeah I know my nose is, but otherwise I'm pretty perfect on paper too: good education with a Bachelor's degree from London, have a regular job, speak Gujarati, Hindi, Marathi and English, have a fair complexion, a petite figure, long, black hair. In reality, I have a crooked nose, average looks, I barely passed my exams and was forced to take this job by my father. I hate taking decisions and my friends describe me as confused, irrational, lazy and unambitious. I can't cook to save my life and hard work isn't my forte. So really, I'm not perfect at all. So shouldn't I actually be looking for a not-so-perfect man to be married to?

'Neha!' Tanya nudges my stomach, jolting me out of my thoughts. 'Where are the press kits?' she urgently whispers while the chief guest's boring speech drones on.

Shit, where did I keep them?

I run around frantically searching for the piles of press kits I was in charge of for the reporters covering tonight's event; the only responsibility given to me for the evening.

Why am I here? I'm of no use. I just stand at the back and do nothing. I can't even keep track of stuff that I have to simply hold!

I find the pile of paper files sitting neatly on a velvet chair at the back of the hall. The weight falls heavy on my small frame as I go in search of Tanya and Nisha.

I look around the convention hall and I finally take notice of the entire show my team has put up. It's a great feat to pull off at such short notice along with the last minute speech drafting, arranging invites, taking care of the press coverage and pulling favours from almost every related department. Well, I didn't really do anything, the team did. I quite detest responsibility; something I blame my sheltered life for since I don't like to take the blame myself. So far nothing in my life has been achieved by my own efforts. My college applications and admission were completed entirely by my pushy and ambitious mother, my job arranged by my dad upon my return after graduation. My life is dictated by my family and friends.

My shopping is done by my mother. And, at twenty-five, my parents are now in charge of finding me a husband too, which is how I met Rajesh.

Work events are incredibly boring and the only area of interest to me is the bar. I always wish I could drink during these events; Harry insists on only the best alcohol in town.

Fat chance of getting a drop of alcohol here. I mean, since I don't really contribute to the work, the least I can do is stay sober!

Harry darling hosts extravagant parties at the drop of the hat. Every small announcement made by his firm turns into a page three party. For his last decadence we had to fly in Ukrainian dancers to welcome the guests. I often wonder how his stakeholders feel about such immoderate expenses eating into their dividends. His tiny frame struggles to hold up his larger-than-life belly while his receding hairline shouts out his old age. White pants, white shirt and white shoes, accessorized with chains of gold, rings on every finger and a shiny gold and diamond-studded Rolex completes his look.

Tonight Monica is wearing a revealing gown which offers splendid views of her voluptuous assets as she seductively poses in front of the paparazzi. Her caked up face shows off a well-rehearsed smile.

Bored from standing uselessly at the back I take a trip to the bathroom. Tanya, drained from the hectic day's work since she is the real star at office, is fixing her hair. I'm not drained, I'm just bored.

I stand next to her to examine my appearance. My reflection is a sorry sight. Tanya, at 5'7" stands tall without a trace of fatigue showing through her make-up. I slouch even at 5'1" and appear exhausted and worn out. My fair skin looks pale despite the greasepaint and my tired eyes are puffy and swollen, further attracting attention to my biggest visual flaw: my protruding nose! I hate my nose. I have always wanted to get it fixed but the fear of needles overpowered my mission a few years ago. And so I have learned to accept it. Or rather, ignore it.

Sigh. Darling Rajesh would definitely have made a comment tonight if he saw me!

Beep: It's Rajesh.

'Hi baby, will I get to talk to you tonight? I miss you.'

My heart skips a beat. I reply: 'Hi, yes, but I'm gonna be late.'

He responds instantly: 'How much longer though? It's almost midnight.'

I text back: 'I'll try calling, or else we'll talk tomorrow,' and stuff my phone into my bag.

Okay, so I need some space. But I do like him. I mean I don't feel like vomiting at the mere thought of him. At least, not yet. So, perhaps he is the one?

Beep. It's Sanya: 'Bloody hell. I just got stuck in a lift with four guys and not one of them was bangable. What has the world come to?'

I giggle, shaking my head. Girlfriends always know how to perk up a dreary night!

Rita enters the washroom with a stern face and announces, 'Neha, where are the press kits? Why haven't you handed them out yet?' and storms out.

How hard can this 'most important task for Neha' be? But I can't help thinking that I should really be at a bar right now with Palak, Lara and Sanya. Staying sober does not bode me well.

Tonight's so-called red-carpet event comprises a lavish display of hors d'oeuvres and an open bar; recession hasn't really affected the city's party habits. The open bar is the most important part of any event. It is hardly surprising that half of Mumbai comes to such incredibly boring events purely for the free booze and for the page three exposure in the *Bombay Times*. They usually head straight to the bar and only once loaded with some expensive imported whisky and scrumptious shrimp canapés topped with truffle oil, will they head towards the hosts and compliment them on a good party; that is, before venturing towards friends to backbite on how the host is a big scamster or to complain about the missing caviar on the menu! Conversations can be overheard about basically nothing relevant or remotely intelligent. From women of every age you hear just a lot of 'dah-lings' and 'babes' while they pick on the hors d'oeuvres (note: they do not eat them; however else will they fit into the latest Pucci dress!).

Tanya motions to me whilst I struggle to walk around in search of reporters and journalists with the heavy pile of files in my hands.

She whispers, 'They are here again.'

I turn with difficulty to look in the direction Tanya points at. At the back of the hall stand four grimacing men in tattered jeans, cheap shiny shirts and chains. They look relatively frightening and menacing, even more so against the elegant backdrop. Guests passing by gasp at this intimidating sight and maintain a distance. Tanya and I watch as one of the ruffians, possibly the leader of the gang, walks threateningly to an unaware Harry darling.

Harry turns around smiling widely at the firm hand on his shoulder, expecting an old friend. As soon as he sets eyes on his 'friend', his smile quickly vanishes and his eyes widen as his stout frame held up by suspenders shakes uncontrollably. From where I am standing I can see his white shirt starting to soak up the sweat. Onlookers stare rudely, trying to catch a word or two of their conversation. Rita appears without delay and gently drags them to the side, away from the public glare. A few heated words are exchanged. Harry darling is seen pleading and begging with his hands, still sweating profusely while Rita tries to play the intermediary. The *tapori* walks off, followed by his three sidekicks.

I look around for Monica but she is oblivious of her husband's predicament as she sips on her tenth glass of champagne while her neckline creeps down, showing more than necessary.

Tanya and I exchange conspiratorial glances; this is the third time the *gunda*s have come to his public events. There are rumours that his 'Colombian drug money' is combined with heavy borrowings from a local moneylender. And these rogues definitely look like they are the street mafia! Perhaps the rumours are true. Maybe that's why he always insists on throwing these big bashes, to convince his stakeholders that all is well at Harry Constructions Ltd. And he has a demanding wife like Monica to add to his woes!

Y

As I tuck myself into bed my mind switches to Rajesh's messages and my stomach feels wobbly again.

Perhaps he is the one?

In such a short time span, Rajesh and I have become really close (and we kissed!), something very unusual for me. It's scary. When I met him for the first time a few weeks back, it was a humid October day. I thought it would be a quick meeting; he hadn't been able to make much of an impression on me. After the first twenty minutes I was certain that he was not my type; but then again, what is my type? I am twenty-five with a series of bad relationships in my kitty, what do I know about my *type*? I comforted myself in the days after by considering them experiences of life-learning lessons, most of which I try to drown out with booze!

Our first meeting was scheduled for an after-work coffee. Even with my limited expectations from arranged set-ups, at my first glimpse of him, I'd be lying if I said I wasn't disappointed.

He is twenty-eight years old, stands at an average height of 5'10", small built, a faint paunch and slim arms and legs; large eyes stick out disproportionally on his small face. His cheeks are full, hinting at a double chin at times. His smile shows perfectly lined teeth, giving way to faint dimples. But after an initial unpromising 'Hello', he managed to hook me on longer.

He walked over and said, 'Hi, Neha?'

I looked up, smiled and said, 'Yes, Rajesh?'

And we shook hands as we both checked each other out. He was wearing formal work pants with a well-fitted shirt neatly tucked in. His hair was properly combed to the side. *A good Gujarati boy.*

I motioned him to a chair while he asked, 'What will you have? I'm hungry; let's order something to eat too?' We ordered our coffees and sandwiches and got down to the interrogation session.

He peered at me and said, 'Just be yourself. No need to refrain from saying anything.' He was overflowing with confidence and clearly in charge of the conversation.

I smiled back and said, 'Don't worry, I'm fine.'

I wasn't fine, but I had to say so. Actually I am very shy and my weird sense of humour is not always appreciated.

Our cappuccinos arrived and I silently approved as he tore open a packet of Demerara sugar for his coffee; my mother would like him. Conversation flowed smoothly and time passed by rapidly. He seemed interesting and educated on various topics that ranged from the business world, the media, the city, travel, lifestyle and education. I learnt he did his Bachelors in America followed by an MBA in the UK and is currently working in the family business and is pretty content at where he is at the moment.

He stared at my face continuously till I felt he was scrutinizing every pore on my skin; something I really detest. I would rather go unnoticed and blend into the crowd. I abhor attention. Neither have I ever been the central attraction nor have I ever been in a position of any consequence, and I quite like it that way.

I could see that he cared about appearances. I hate first meetings for this very reason. So much gets read into small irrelevant things. And unfortunately, too much emphasis goes into the outside package and hence I am compromised because of my protruding nose—something I am very conscious about. And my height!

Then he brought out specific arranged marriage questions like, 'Are you okay living in a joint family?', 'What do you intend on doing in the future?' and so on. As I replied to his well-memorized questions, I realized that he was rather experienced in 'marriage-meetings'.

It wasn't long before my doubt was cleared as he kept repeating, 'I have rejected many girls because I don't quite like the typical page three kinds or girls who are too materialistic.' I sensed a hint of an inferiority complex and a bruised ego. *Maybe something to do with an ex-girlfriend.*

He was too quick to reply to my question of what he looks for in a girl, 'For some reason I am attracted only to girls who are fair and have long hair.'

I could either show that the comment really pissed me off,

or laugh at the ridiculousness of his shallow mind. I chose to laugh and he mistook it as a sign of 'she agrees'. That's my problem: I don't speak my mind. I let many issues slip by and it's only a matter of time before I burst and run. Luckily I am fair and I do have long hair; I must be blessed.

I also observed him as the conversation flowed; he is slightly egoistic about his status and money, but then so is everyone in snobby SoBo; the fact that he had rejected many marriage proposals also seemed to have boosted his ego. He has led a rather sheltered and spoilt life for which I blame his parents and yes, he lacks some social skills: he licked the butter knife to finish off the remaining pesto from his sandwich.

But I forgivingly overlooked these small issues and considered meeting him a second time. Despite the flaws, I was intrigued by him; after all, I am not perfect either. But even I was a little surprised by my interest in him.

By the time we were done with our coffee it was almost 10 p.m. and I was clueless about what to do next. Thankfully, he jumped in and nervously asked, 'So, Neha, would you like to meet tomorrow for coffee again?'

I smiled back and said 'Yes, I'd like that.'

Since then we had been chatting regularly, meeting often and talking about everything and anything under the sun! He is a hopeless romantic, sweet, charming, caring and he makes me smile. Well, most of the time. In short, he keeps me entertained. But now the question is how *long* can he keep me entertained?

I run at the mention of flowers, candles and chocolates. Okay, maybe not chocolates. There are a lot of hopes riding on me. And everyone is praying that I don't run this time around.

But with Rajesh, things have been different. I have become more tolerant and do not exactly squirm at the mere thought of romance with him.

So should I call him now? He isn't exactly my boyfriend. But he did message me, wanting to talk.

Well, it would be legit to call him since I'm in a kinda-relationship with a promise of it ending in marriage. Quite unbelievable. *And maybe too good to be true?*

Mmm . . . No, let's not get too ahead of ourselves. If I call now, it might establish a boyfriend–girlfriend relationship with a hint that I really am interested, when I am not so sure.

But when will I be sure?

ONE CAN NEVER BE TOO THIN OR TOO RICH

Celebrating a baby shower with such hype doesn't make sense to me, but then again, most of what my society does is not normal. The traditional *godh bharay* (baby shower) ceremony has been replaced with the western baby shower concept with pink and blue ribbons, champagne flutes and anything else picked up from American sitcoms and movies. I don't really understand why one who is not even an acquaintance (like me) has to be invited to an occasion as personal as a baby shower.

My mother looks at me disdainfully as I emerge from the bath and as she examines my skin, her wrinkle-free forehead (thanks to generous doses of Botox) attempts to crease up. Her fair and luminous face is a stark contrast to my dull, tired and puffy-eyed face.

'Why can't you take more care of yourself? How many times will you reschedule your facial appointments? Can't you take some inspiration from Sanya? Look at her, always so well turned out. She always has her hair blown out, her face is free of blemishes and she always applies a sun-screen lotion before leaving the house. Why can't you follow her footsteps?'

'Mum, stop it, I don't want to go to the stupid baby shower. I don't even know whose it is.'

'Neha, stop being childish, you need to be seen. There will be plenty of mothers who have single sons. So start getting ready and look your best. And you do know the hosts; its Leena *kaki*'s son-in-law's sister who is pregnant!'

Oh, of course we know them.

Everyone knows everyone and everyone is somehow related, unless of course the guy is smart or rich or anything else that makes him an eligible bachelor.

'You're wearing the new anarkali with this jewellery and please for God's sake use that hair iron I got you. You look terrible!'

My mother points out the clothes and jewellery neatly laid out on my bed, complete with matching shoes and purse. That's my mother for you; a stickler for appearances. She has been fretting over my marriage since the day I turned sixteen. And now that I am a single twenty-five-year-old, she turns hysterical each time someone's engagement is announced, worrying that her daughter may never marry. She had even started reading up on mutual funds and other investing instruments to guarantee a secure financial future for me in case I never marry and end up all alone.

On her way out of my room she shouts, 'Use the concealer liberally, darling, you need it. And put some bronzer on the nose!'

So, after generous dollops of concealer, foundation and blush, I look fairly presentable in an anarkali outfit, a pista-green shade which perfectly complements my fair skin, and superficially flushed cheeks, courtesy MAC.

At the moment Rajesh is a blurry presence in my mind. I try with all my might to ignore the uneasiness but it continues to linger.

'Neha, here, pink lipstick!,' shouts my mother from her room.

Seriously, what part of her genes have I inherited?

My mother appears in the doorway with a lipstick in her hand, dressed in a glitzy pink embroidered sari with diamonds adding more lustre to her weekly facialled skin.

The world must wonder how I am related to her.

'I gotta feeling . . . Tonight's gonna be a good night . . .'

Rajesh's name blinks on my BlackBerry screen as it rings.

What shall I do? No, I am not in the mood to talk to him right now. I'll deal with him later.

'Tonight's gonna be a good, good night . . .' my phone continues to ring, as I stare at the screen.

Five minutes after I ignored his call I receive a BBM from Rajesh:

'Hi baby, tried calling. Hope you had a good day at work. Call me when you free, I wanna hear your voice.'

I can't help but smile.

Y

Arriving at any high society function is like walking into a bull ring wearing a red T-shirt. Despite having attended these dos regularly for twenty-five years, I still have not become immune to the pretentious show. It does not matter how close your 'friends' are, they are women; just because you are a vegetarian does not mean the bull won't charge at you!

And the entry is the worst. People start discussing you the moment you walk in, including your outfit, jewellery, shoes, purse, hair, face, and your escort for the night. It doesn't end there: when and where was the dress repeated before, which store sold it, when it went on sale, and how much it ultimately cost with the discount is discussed. Of course, any previous scandals and gossip linked to you is also brought up and incessantly whispered about until the next target arrives.

So as is customary, when I arrive, I am thoroughly scrutinized, particularly due to my single status. I always end up feeling judged, criticized and thoroughly analysed. Mumbai hosts an intricately interlinked Gujarati and Jain society; it is filled with aunties keen on knowing whose daughter is doing what and whose son is doing who. They are overflowing with the latest gossip and on more than a few occasions I receive updates on my former classmates from my mother's wide network of friends, kakis, *masi*s and *mami*s!

Palak is always my saviour at these dos as she is also dragged into this society by her parents. She always manages to find me, pull me away and give me some of the booze from her mini flask.

But right now, I can't find her in this humungous hall decorated ostentatiously with flowers, ribbons and beads hanging from every corner. Women are dressed in every shade of the rainbow and some more, with huge rocks dripping from their ears, necks and wrists.

At my baby shower I will have shades of silver, pink and blue balloons and ribbons for my baby. And none of this 'over the top' nonsense; just a small gathering of family and friends and lots and lots of gifts! And a big chocolate cake! But . . . who's baby will I be having?

The thought depresses me. I BBM Palak: 'Where the hell are you? S.O.S.'

Instead, a fat old aunty comes to air kiss me and forcefully leads me to a round table seated by even rounder, well-coiffed-up ladies, decked to the nines in sleeveless blouses showing off their mammoth arms. Sometimes fashion manages to do some pretty terrible things to people. Lara would definitely suffer a heart attack here.

'*Yeh rahi Neha!*' exclaims Hideous Aunty No. 1.

'Neha, where is your beautiful mother?' asks Hideous Aunty No. 2, to which I shrug.

Each hippo on the table X-rays me from top to bottom while I stand there uncomfortably, scanning the room for Palak.

Tonight is Hideous Aunty No. 3's turn to bitch me out, 'Neha, you must get married soon, I see some grey hair already, you're getting old now.'

What the . . .

I stand there aghast and horrified at her rudeness and am about to hit back about her flabby elephant arms when a hand squeezes my shoulder.

Palak from behind says, 'There you are, Neha, come on, all the young people are on that side. Stop socializing with the oldies, you have a good fifty years to get to this table! Come on now, love.' Palak smirks at them and turns me around and leads me to a far corner. The large ladies sit there (they can't quite stand up in time) with their mouths open, frowning in indignation.

'Thank you!' I try to laugh but am still wincing from the comment.

Palak giggles, 'That was fun! Bloody old hags, they should see their ugly faces in the mirror before picking on someone else!'

Palak walks expertly in her tightly wrapped mauve chiffon sari (her favourite colour!) dodging the little brats running around and touching the feet of other old hags as required. I, on the other hand, manage to bump into every unattended chair, table and flying kid around me. We reach a corner when Palak opens her Fendi purse to reveal a silver flask.

'Here, quickly,' she passes the flask to me.

'I better not get any shit for this,' I open it and smell the vodka mixed with soda.

'Are you kidding me? The other kids are smoking pot outside,' she giggles and then turns serious. 'So I heard something unpleasant about Sanya.'

'Uh oh, what?' I worry as I take a few swigs.

'It's about her and Sanjay. Some people have been saying things. There has been a rumour about them seeing each other.'

'She did stay in that night waiting for him to call. I have no idea why, and she isn't saying anything.'

'Yes, she has been acting really secretive lately,' Palak raises her eyebrows above her delicate rimless frame.

'Well, what are we supposed to do? What *can* we do? And especially when she hasn't said anything to us?'

'I'm gonna bring it up with her,' Palak says determinedly. 'This is just ridiculous. She will ruin her life over him. He isn't just any guy. He is bloody married. Nothing will happen to him.' She clenches her jaws.

'What if she just denies the whole thing? You know, we all look so stupid when the whole world is whispering something and we have no idea what the truth is. We can't even defend her,' I am pissed off.

'I don't know. By the way, another bit of bad news for you. Some people have heard about you and Rajesh already.'

'What? How?' I ask surprised.

How does anyone know? And where does Palak get all this gossip from?

'Well, you went to Amadeus, Neha. What do you expect?'

'Argh! Someone must have seen us. Why are people so nosy?'

'And, Natasha knows about it,' Palak warns. She had done her research well: according to the local grapevine Natasha and Rajesh had been seeing each other.

I stare at her, stunned and confused, 'What do I do though? Rajesh hasn't even mentioned her name. Did they go out for long?'

'I don't know. But she is here and she knows. So just stay alert.'

Oh shit. I hate dealing with such sensitive shit, especially when I have nothing to do with it.

I quickly gulp down the rest of what's left in the flask to gear me up. And then go in search for food.

We bump into my mother and she squeals at Palak, 'Palak! How are you? You look gorgeous in a sari! I keep telling Neha to become a little more like the rest of you girls, but it is just impossible!'

'Thank you, Aunty.'

'Neha! Why is your face so red?' she frowns. She takes out a compact powder from her purse and pats my face. I smile as the vodka kicks into my system.

'I'm hungry,' I whine.

'Neha, eat healthy. Palak, please watch out for this girl,' she calls out as she walks away.

Palak laughs and takes me towards the buffet table. She picks up some salad and grilled tikkas, while I load my plate with cocktail samosas and wontons.

'Have you spoken to Rajesh properly yet though?' she asks in a lowered voice.

'Nah,' I say.

'Shh, Neha, speak softly,' she says sternly.

'Well, I don't know, I'm kind of embarrassed to see him. What do I say? I can't face him right now,' I say through bites of the hot samosa.

'Has he called or texted?'

'Yeah, both, but I don't really answer properly either.'

'Neha!'

'What? Fine! I will call him but later at night. When I go back.'

Someone taps me on the shoulder.

'So, I hear you're dating Rajesh,' a woman says from behind.

I turn around bewildered. And I freeze. It's Natasha.

'Excuse me?' I ask in indignation.

'All I have to say is good luck!' she snorts.

'What?' I raise my voice fearlessly, thanks to the few swigs of vodka.

'Oh please, word gets around fast. I will always know who you are shacking up with!'

'Who the hell do you think you are? And what's your *fucking* problem?' I retort angrily.

'I don't have any problem, I'm just warning you.' Natasha flips her Rihanna haircut to the side and purposely brushes past me, casually tipping her drink. Her hideous red-coloured mocktail spills onto my pale green georgette dupatta.

'What the . . .'

Palak grabs me and pulls me to the side to avoid a scene amongst the inquisitive eyes and ears.

'What . . . was . . . that?' I ask stunned.

'You just got bitchslapped!' Palak responds in shock, her eyes look even bigger through her glasses.

'How embarrassing!' I exclaim, quite shaken. 'And how dare she, that bitch!'

'It's okay, relax. But why do you think that things didn't work out between them?'

'No idea. But whatever the reason, she does *not* need to pour her drink on me!'

'It seems like he dumped her!'

'She is fair and pretty. I think those are his only two requirements,' I roll my eyes.

'She is very headstrong. As you can see!' she laughs. 'Maybe that's why? He wants someone who isn't that wild.' She raises her eyebrow, 'So, are you docile or are you wild?'

'Shut up,' I grumble and I stuff another warm samosa into my mouth. The hot, spicy and crunchy treat comforts me a little.

'She so did that on purpose, bloody bitch,' I still fret and fume.

'Neha, I think you really need to talk to him about a few things. I'm bringing this up because I think you like him and I have a feeling you might get sucked in too deep without realizing how much you are compromising,' she lectures.

Sure I have a mind of my own and I am not docile. But I am definitely not wild or feral. Sanya is wild. Not me. Neither is Palak. But it doesn't mean we are tame or docile. We are smart and sassy. Yes Neha, you are smart. And sassy.

As soon as I reach home I receive another text: 'Where are you, baby? Is everything okay?'

Are you crazy? Everything is wrong. Why on earth would anyone say something like that to someone? How dare that bitch come and confront me like that! Shit, why do I always react so late? Why couldn't I have said something nasty to her face? Am I docile now?

I call him straightaway. My anxiety and nervousness evaporates and is replaced by anger and humiliation.

'Hi Neha, where have you been? Are you okay?' Rajesh says as he picks up.

'I went for a baby shower and a girl who knows about us, came up to me. The bitch actually warned me about you. She said, "All I have to say is good luck!" And then that whore poured her drink on me on purpose!' I fume, unable to keep my anger in control.

'What? Who said that?' he asks baffled.

'Natasha!'

'Natasha?' he bursts out laughing. 'Oh God, she is just jealous of you, that's all.' And then he adds, 'She wanted to marry me but I didn't want to.'

'*She* wanted to marry you?' I ask in disbelief.

'Yes.'

'Wha-? You used to actually date her?'

'Well, no.' He sounds uncomfortable.

'Rajesh, will you tell me the truth?'

'Okay, our parents set us up and I just didn't like her.'

'Why?'

'I don't know, Neha! I just didn't really like her. But she was all over me!' he laughs.

'That's it? You didn't like her? She is fair and pretty!' I say sarcastically. The vodka is still running in my blood.

'Pretty? No way! She has short hair! That is just *sooo* unattractive!'

I pause.

'What?' I ask slowly.

'I don't think she is pretty.'

'Because of her haircut?'

'No! I just don't think she is pretty. I am entitled to an opinion, Neha!'

'Were you a total jerk to her? Because why else would someone react like that?'

'No, I wasn't. She messaged me a few times and I just didn't reply. So maybe that's why she is pissed. She is just jealous of you because you have me. Her parents were really eager for her to marry me. But I said no,' he boasts proudly. 'And I can't be forced. And I didn't like her. She has a really sharp tongue and has a completely different outlook on life. I prefer it if the girl and I share similar tastes so she likes whatever I pick out.'

Excuse me?

'So you basically want everything your way? You cannot compromise at all?' I ask sceptically. The vodka is still there, boiling away.

'Neha, why are you arguing? These are such small things. I am a good guy for you. You are lucky.'

I am lucky? Who does he think he is?

But I give up, I'm too tired. 'So tell me something else that I don't know. I'd like to have some fair warning before I get embarrassed again,' I say sarcastically.

He doesn't pick up on the hint. 'Don't worry, it won't happen again,' he says confidently. 'So, how many guys were hitting on you there?'

'Oh, shut up.' I smile again.

ALL THAT GLITTERS ISN'T GOLD

There are times when one needs an outlet. Each day has its share of moments, but there are some days which are filled with so many moments that by the end very little tolerance level remains. Today has been my moment-filled day. And I have a strong feeling that no amount of alcohol is going to get rid of the bitter aftertaste.

No, Neha, get up. It cannot be like this any more. It's time to take charge of your life and look forward. No more over analysing, just go out and be optimistic. Be positive. But this time, I will not let Rajesh say what he wants and get away with it. I repeat that over and over again in my mind.

※

'*I gotta feeling . . .*'

'Hmm . . .' I grunt into my phone.

'Hold on, sunshine! Palak is on conference,' Lara chuckles.

'Hmm . . .'

'Bad day?'

'Horrible!'

'We were wondering what to do about Sanya,' Palak updates me.

My mind is too drained to discuss Sanya's alleged liaison with the married jerk.

'I think we should put Sanya on our conference call and speak to her together. If we physically confront her, she'll feel even more cornered,' says Lara.

'Yeah, okay,' agrees Palak.

'Are you sure about Sanya getting into someone else's car last weekend, Palak?' I ask.

'Yes, I am sure,' butts in Lara. 'Vick wasn't drunk at all, and come on, we can all spot Sanya from a mile away. Even Ashish has heard whispers about her and Sanjay.'

'Oh man! Okay, Palak, call her,' I say.

Sanya joins the conference.

'Hello!'

'Sanya!' commands Palak in her authoritative tone.

'Uh oh, am I gonna get a lecture? What did I do?' whines Sanya.

'Hi Sanya, Lara is here too,' I pipe in.

'Ooh, hello, it's a conference! What's up guys?' she coos.

'Sanya, there are a few rumours going around,' says Palak delicately.

'About?' Sanya already sounds defensive.

'About you and Sanjay,' replies an angry Lara. 'What is going on? Is there something we should know?'

'What? Me and Sanjay?' Sanya laughs. 'Guys, there is nothing!'

'Then why are people wagging their tongues? There is never any fire without fuel,' I say.

'Well we've met a few times at events and you know, he is all flirtatious and so am I. People are just applying and overworking their imagination. And I am not infatuated with him at all. Sure he's easy on the eyes and a smooth talker, but remember it's me! It takes much more than that to sway me,' she laughs.

The three of us remain silent. We aren't convinced.

'Sanya, you have been acting shady for a while. Disappearing every now and then, arriving late, leaving early, evading questions,' Lara points out.

'Yeah Sanya, and since when do you ever stay home at night? You are a socialite, nothing can keep you home, unless there is a man in question,' adds Palak.

'Guys, really, thank you all for being so concerned, but honestly, I am not doing anything stupid. I have not even considered it.'

'Sanya, if you are looking for a fling, a married guy is not a good choice,' I chip in.

'STOP! I am not looking for a fling. I am not with Sanjay. I appreciate the concern and worry, but I am really not doing anything wrong. We are just friends,' she insists, her voice rising a little.

She is clearly upset. Not just angry. That's not like Sanya at all.

'Okay fine, we believe you. We just kept hearing this and we were really worried. And now we know how to answer with conviction if anyone says anything,' says Lara.

'Thank you. I am saying the truth. We are *just* friends,' Sanya repeats earnestly.

I am so not convinced. She was flustered when I asked about her plans last week, her voice is shaky over the phone, and she is not fuming as expected which can only mean she is guilty.

'Sanya, just know that we are here for you if you ever need anything,' I say quietly. 'And really think things through before you do anything.'

'Okay, thank you, but this really is unnecessary,' she grumbles.

'Okay, sorry Sanya, we just wanted to make sure. All right, can we go to Aer on Friday night? All of us? We'll ask the guys too,' asks Palak to lighten things up.

'Ooh yes! Neha, do you think you wanna bring Rajesh?' asks Lara.

'Hmm . . . actually, maybe I should,' I ponder out loud.

'Yes! Yes!' squeals Sanya.

'Okay, done, so Friday night at Aer. Neha and her frog will be coming too!' Palak giggles.

'Yes, me and my frog!' I laugh. 'Okay, I have to go get ready now, I'm meeting him for dinner. Bye guys, see you Friday!'

🍸

While waiting for Rajesh, I smile with anticipation, excited about a good meal with him. I had taken the effort to get ready: worn a short black dress, applied make-up and yes, I even used the hair straightener! I'm feeling good. I have forgotten the Natasha incident. Well almost; it is difficult to erase the humiliating drink spill!

He picks me up in one of his fancy cars and as I slide into the front seat eager to hear a compliment, his first words are, 'You're wearing black!'

My crisis returns.

I've been up since the ungodly hour of 6 a.m., prancing around a truckload of dumb and dumbers at work, generally pissed off at the world. But since Rajesh had insisted I wear a dress, I shaved my legs in a jiffy, cutting myself twice, just so I could wear a stupid damn dress and high heels to boot: and yet I have to hear this crap?

When Rajesh had called earlier I had been tempted to avoid the dinner date, but he insisted and the thought of being alone at night drove me to say yes. He had promised an early night. And as the evening drew closer my hesitation began to turn into anticipation. I had been looking forward to an evening with just the two of us, and some good food of course!

But (there is always a *but*) instead, I now want to punch the freaking daylights out of him.

Be positive.

I take a deep breath, smile, and say, 'Yes, I'm wearing black, I just want to have some good food and wine and sleep soundly tonight.'

He smiles back with a hint of satisfaction; maybe he likes the fact that I don't snap back. He takes my hand as he drives towards the Oberoi Trident and he twirls my fingers playfully. He looks at me, then towards our joined hands; he notices my pink nails and his smile disappears.

He frowns, 'Ugh, this is such a loud colour. Please remove it!'

For the first time in my life I do not have a polite answer. I muster up every bit of restraint to hold back from snapping at him; I manage to remain silent, pretending not to hear. But I should've known better. Not wise enough to take the hint and being persistent, Rajesh continues on the subject of nail polish and manicures. I just found a male version of Sanya.

Why is he so obsessed with appearances? He has no right to talk; he looks just like a frog! And I have already kissed him and there are still no signs of him turning into a prince. Am I going to drown in the lake with this dumb toad?

By the time we reach the hotel, I am super pissed and grumpy. But he is so self-involved in nail polish shades, dresses and fashion, he fails to notice my silence.

If only he could read my mind.

Rajesh leads me to Indiana Jones, strutting with arrogant confidence. I prefer to stand behind him as the maitre d' eyes Rajesh from top to bottom and nods politely. Rajesh's ego balloon bursts.

He brusquely announces, 'I have a reservation, Rajesh Parikh.'

'This way,' the maitre d' replies indifferently.

He leads us through the restaurant to a corner table, passing over the small waterbody with lilies. This is one my favourite restaurants and their dishes make it to my list of comfort food. When the maitre d' seats us, he looks at me carefully, noticing me for the first time, and recognizes me instantly.

His disgruntled mood changes immediately, 'Oh hello, young lady, I am so sorry I didn't see you behind the gentleman. How is your father? It's been a while since we saw you here!' he says delightfully.

I smile back, grateful for a friendly face and smile even wider when I catch Rajesh's surprised look that soon turns glum when the maitre d' asks, 'So will it be the usual for you? And what about your *friend*?' emphasizing on 'friend' with distaste.

'Umm, let's have a look at the menu, but I'm sure I'm going to stick to the usual,' I laugh.

'Certainly,' he bows slightly and leaves, but not before glancing at Rajesh with suspicion.

He clearly has strong judgements about people.

'So you come here often?' Rajesh asks sombrely.

'Yes, I love this place. Actually, let me do the ordering today, you can pick out the wine.'

He agrees hesitantly.

He's probably worrying about the bill.

While I skim through the menu making quick decisions, he pours over the wine list, blatantly checking out the prices. *Gentlemen's etiquette at its best!* These are the warning signals I should watch out for but I am too famished and grumpy to care right now.

I motion the waiter to place my order, aware that Rajesh is going to take time. The maitre d' arrives at our table instead to take our order. I ask for chicken spring rolls, papaya salad and Chilean sea bass, side of greens and steamed rice. I do not even bother to ask Rajesh if it is okay.

The maitre d' gives me an acknowledging smile since my order is my usual. 'Very well, ma'am.'

'Please bring the starters soon. I am hungry, and he'll take time to decide on the wine,' I look apologetically towards him.

'Very well, ma'am. Sir, may I suggest a good bottle to you?'

'Mmm,' Rajesh ponders, scrutinizing the wine list.

'Let me place your food order and I can come back,' the maitre d' says politely.

Rajesh takes another embarrassing eight minutes to decide upon the wine. He asks to see five various bottles and to taste each one putting on a bit of a show, I presume for my benefit, and finally chooses the 'right one' (undeniably by the price).

Bored with his one-sided conversation on wines, I look around to do some people watching, and my gaze stops abruptly at the entrance when Reema walks in.

Reema is the biggest gossip bitch in SoBo, and most people dread the sight of her; super obnoxious, super interfering and super rude. She never thinks before speaking and has no reservations on asking the strangest and most personal of questions to just about anyone. Once, very randomly, she asked Lara at a party on what contraception she used and whether she does Brazilian wax for her beau or not. She even looks scary; she is rather large, hideous and vulgar. She possesses the biggest hips, and she makes it a point to wear low necklines to flaunt her drooping breasts. She is a sorry sight for all. It is common knowledge that people tend to change directions when they catch sight of her. Today she is without her two sidekicks, Reshma and Mona, who are equally rude, obnoxious and large; but Reema overshadows them with the largest butt! And she is by far the bitchiest.

She walks into the restaurant like she owns the world, her large hips swaying from side to side. She catches my eye and returns my gaze with a stony stare, eyes Rajesh from top to toe and walks on.

Crap! Now it's really going to be all over town!

Our conversation starts to flow onto various topics such as our work, his business activities, funny clients and I tell him about Harry darling and Monica the Bitch. He pretends to pay attention but I know he's not listening.

The starters arrive and I dive into the spring rolls. Fried food always makes everything all right.

'On Friday my friends are going to Aer for drinks. I'd like it if you come. You'll get to meet them and they'll know that I am not dating someone imaginary!' I say as I pop my second spring roll into my mouth.

'Ah, so you want to introduce me to your friends?'

'Well, I am just saying, you know. I think it's okay for them to meet you,' I am starting to feel red. 'Reema just walked in right now and saw us together, so I guess the whole town will know by midnight anyways,' I add.

Rajesh shrugs his shoulders indifferently, 'I really don't care about her. I always make sure I stay away from such dumb socialites and anyone who associates with them. They are so materialistic and shallow.' He goes on a raging spree about the page three society of Mumbai, touches upon the subject of the film industry and finally, about the restaurant's food. I only hear bits and pieces in between my spring rolls, papaya salad and wine.

The main course arrives and I want another bottle of wine to have with my sea bass; Rajesh counts the calorie content of the dishes while raving about the excellent wine which is 'Indian made and so cheap'.

Where on earth has he learnt his chivalry from?

I resist the urge to record my conversation to bitch about him with my friends. They would've eaten him alive for sure! As he drones on about nonsensical things I keep asking myself: *Why, why, why?*

How will I survive when it takes me every bit of my willpower to stop yelling at him? Do I have to make these many compromises? I'm getting sick of him already and we've only known each other for a month.

'I'm happy you wore a dress,' he comments. 'Even though it's black.'

'You're welcome,' I remark dryly, with a smile. *I don't think anything he says or does will help now.*

'See, we should do things for each other if it makes us happy or pleases the other.'

Really?

He smiles endearingly.

'So, today at work, *Femina* magazine came in to interview my boss, Rita. They are doing a feature on women achievers.'

'Oh,' he frowns and then scrutinizes me. 'That's nice, but,' he leans closer and narrows his eyes, 'please don't become a feminist. On one hand you demand chivalry, on the other you want equal rights!'

Chivalry? What chivalry does he have anyways?

I have no choice but to give him a fake smile. There isn't a drop of energy left in me to fight back. Stuffed to the core, I can no longer eat and slightly buzzing from two bottles of wine,

I am ready to go home and sleep. It had not been a good day nor has it been a good date. The highlight of the day, the food, is comforting and the wine is doing its job. The dinner is not exactly going as well as I had expected, and I give myself some leeway: tonight is not a night to make a decision on Rajesh.

Rajesh asks, 'Up for some dessert?'

Shaking my head, I decline, 'No sorry, I am too full.'

'But you have to have some with me,' he whines.

I firmly shake my head again. 'No sweetie, I am counting calories,' I reply sugar sweetly, patting my stomach.

The cheque arrives and I don't bother offering to pay. On the way out, we pass by Reema's table and I don't dare to look, acknowledge, wave or nod at her.

Thank heavens I'm so buzzed!

On our way out, the maitre d' smiles warmly at me, 'It was great to have you, Neha, I hope you enjoyed your meal?'

'Yes I did, thank you very much.'

Rajesh is about to open his mouth to say something, but the maitre d' looks over him and grunts. Rajesh shuts up, places his hand around my shoulder to throw his weight around, and in a huff, forcefully leads me up the staircase towards the lobby. In my fairly drunken stupor, I start giggling in amusement.

'Why are you laughing?' Rajesh asks angrily.

'Ahem, nothing,' I clear my throat.

I spot only a few people are around. I am in no mood to make small talk with anyone. Especially with Rajesh's arm around me! I recognize nobody after a quick blurry scan.

Once we are out of the protective maitre d's watchful eyes, I abruptly turn around to face Rajesh, placing my palms on his chest. As I open my mouth to say something, a young woman walks past with strong perfume, a familiar scent that catches my breath. I look over Rajesh's shoulders to catch a glimpse of the person, but the woman continues walking towards the elevators without glancing back.

Sanya? Who else catwalks in tight skirts like that? And leaves a strong trail of perfume behind? Could it be a midnight rendezvous with Mr Married?

'Sanya!' I call out. The woman continues walking.

'What happened?'

'Nothing, maybe the wine is making me see things,' I mutter, shaking my head. I concentrate back on Rajesh, 'Wait, you didn't answer me. Will you come on Friday with me to Aer and see my friends?' I lean closer towards his chest.

His face lights up and he pretends to think, 'Mmm . . . I'll think about it.'

'What?' I grumble, and gently hit him with my small clutch bag. He ducks and holds me closer and says, 'Yes, I will come.' Then he smiles and bends down to kiss me, and I step back quickly, 'Not in public,' I gasp wide-eyed.

'Then where?' he whispers into my ear.

'Oye, come on,' I blush.

He starts laughing, the same charming laugh that had attracted me initially.

Maybe it isn't such a bad night after all: good food and wine with a guy who likes me, followed by a goodnight kiss.

EVERY HERO BECOMES A BORE IN THE END

It is finally Friday. My mornings generally start off with a call or a message from Rajesh. Today's message reads: 'Been trying to get you out of my mind but you keep crawling back. Mwah.'

My eyes jolt wide open from my morning dreariness.

Tonight is the night Rajesh will meet everyone.

I take a deep breath and I reply before starting my day: 'Mwah. Can't wait to see you tonight.'

Nisha rushes into work late, flustered and blushing, and drops a bombshell: she is engaged.

We stare at her in shock. *Engaged?* She is the youngest and the quietest in our office, and not to mention, she only graduated recently. Where did a boyfriend come from? While we bombard her with questions of what, how, when and who, she beams coyly and tells us her love story. It was an arranged deal when she and Arjun met a few times and both instantly decided that they were meant for each other. It was as simple as that. Serendipity.

One look at Nisha's blushing face and I could not resist giving her a big hug; I had never seen her so happy.

'You met him just a few times? That's it?' Nisha nods in

response. 'But . . . but . . . how? How did you decide so fast?' I ask flabbergasted.

'Well, I don't know, it just felt right. And whenever I think of him, I smile. I don't need more time to think about it. Don't you feel like that about Rajesh?'

I stare at her with a stunned look.

Feel? Rajesh? Love?

'Umm, well not . . . really . . . yet . . . I mean I barely know him,' I stammer.

Have I ever felt anything for him?

Nisha glows, 'Well, the day you feel and smile like me, you should know he is the one. I don't think it really matters how well you know someone if you feel a connection.'

When the commotion, details and the oohs and aahs over Nisha's announcement settle down, Rita, who is genuinely smiling (a rare occasion), pronounces, 'Come on now, move along and finish up some work. I return to my desk and glance over at Nisha. She is still smiling adorably! I realize there is really such a thing as instant connection.

Do I ever smile like that? Have I ever been as happy as Nisha looks right now?

I think of Rajesh, and then look over at Nisha. I feel uneasy, confused and . . .

No, I don't feel nearly as happy as her. I am not blushing nor am I smiling.

What Nisha has is love. What I have is need. It feels rather unsettling to realize that I have been spending all my time, energy and patience over someone who doesn't make me blush or bring a smile to my face. Or as Sanya would say, burn my loins! Am I just deluding myself thinking that we are in a real relationship. Am I even close to feeling love for him? Do I glow when I think of Rajesh? But then again do I ever glow? I mean, without the alcohol and the rouge. Trying to figure out my feelings for Rajesh makes my head go round in circles. Is what I am doing right?

Maybe he isn't the one then. Maybe all this 'you should know it' or the 'spark shall come' is actually true after all. But then who on earth came up with this arranged marriage shit anyway. How can anyone just fall blindly in love with a stranger? It is the most preposterous thing! I mean, I don't remotely feel like that about Rajesh now, nor did I when we first met. So maybe everyone does not have to feel this way. Maybe some people don't have a heart. Like me.

Too many maybes.

Why is it that I can never hear my heart when I need to? Why does it always shut down when it is supposed to work? Please God, make tonight go well.

Why does this have to be so complicated? Is it because we are always wondering where we will end up, that we might never find happiness? Can we really go in search of happiness? Can we really see the future? Can we always plan and can things always go by our plans? Can we possibly have everything in our hands to control?

Too many cans.

Neha, tonight should give you the answers.

Y

Getting ready for 'the' night, a strange nausea overcomes me and my nervousness returns. What shall I wear? A dress? And see his reaction once again? Or pants? Or a skirt?

'I gotta feeling . . . tonight's gonna be a good night . . .'

My stomach churns again at the sound of my phone.

'Oh my God, Neha, I can't wait to see your frog! Can I pick on him? Pleeeease Neha?' Sanya squeals into the phone.

'No!'

'Can I tell him all your embarrassing stories?'

'No!'

'Come on, relax, I'll just ask all the questions that you've been wanting to ask, like how kinky do you like your girl to be in bed?'

'Shut up, Sanya! Tell me, what should I wear?'

'A skanky dress! By the way, I will see you there because I have to go somewhere else first.'

'Hmm . . . okay,' I murmur, picking out a short grey A-line dress.

When Rajesh picks me up, he gapes at my legs, 'That is short!'

I smile calmly, 'It's my lucky dress! I want my friends to like you!'

'You need luck for that? Why won't they like me just like that?'

'I hope they do,' I quip.

'Are your friends really that important?'

I look at him in surprise, 'Of course they are. They are my best friends!'

He snorts, 'But you should make your own decisions, not ones based on your friends' judgements.'

'Rajesh, I hope you don't hate my friends before meeting them,' I warn.

'No, but I don't know why you are making them out to be so important. This is between you and me, not them.'

'Rajesh, calm down, relax.'

Has he always been so grumpy? Or is this a recent development?

The rest of the drive to the Four Seasons Hotel is spent in silence. A thirty-minute silent trip.

By the time we enter the rooftop bar, the others have already reached.

'Neha!' shouts Raj, waving from the bar. He hugs me and then looks over at Rajesh, 'Hi, I'm Raj,' and they shake hands. 'Come on this side, I think we may get a table there. By the way, Ishaan, Vick and Abhi are also here.'

We follow him to the other section and find Lara, Ashish, Sanya and Palak. They wave excitedly and watch Rajesh with hawk eyes as we walk towards them.

Raj whispers to Rajesh, 'Good luck with the girls. They intend to eat you alive tonight!' he laughs. A frowning Rajesh grunts in response. Everyone buzzes around us and take their fair share of pickings on Rajesh.

Sanya scrutinizes him from top to bottom and says, 'So you really aren't imaginary after all!'

Rajesh's eyes pop out even more in his discomfort.

'Come on, let's get you two a drink,' lightens Lara, fighting the crowd to get to the bar.

On the way to the bar, everyone gets stopped somewhere or the other when bumping into an old acquaintance, friend or colleague. Everyone, except Rajesh. He stands behind me each time I exchange pleasantries with someone. Palak finally grabs and drags me towards the bar with Rajesh following in tow. Sanya, Vick and Abhi are waiting for us there. After the hugs and kisses, I introduce Rajesh to the guys.

Ishaan appears from the crowd and looks at Rajesh and then at me. He smiles brightly and hugs me, 'Hello, Neha!' and plops a kiss on my cheek.

'Hello, Ishaan, no hot model tonight?'

'Of course there is! Hang on a few seconds, she'll be here soon,' he winks at me. 'Hi, I'm Ishaan, and you must be Rajesh?' he smiles warmly.

'Yes,' Rajesh mutters and shakes Ishaan's extended hand. Rajesh clearly doesn't like anyone.

'What will you have to drink? How about a shot for all of us first?' Before anyone can reply, he leans over the bar and orders a round of kamikazes.

Rajesh stares at the shot and I gently nudge him, 'What's wrong?'

'Isn't it too soon to be having shots?' he whispers.

'Oye, this is how we roll!' I hiss.

We toast to a good night of partying and down it.

'Okay, drinks now. What is everyone drinking?' asks Vick.

'Gin and tonic for me, Neha and Sanya,' says Palak.

'No, make it vodka tonic with Grey Goose,' I correct.

'Yeah, perfect.'

Rajesh grabs my arm, 'That's such a manly drink!' he says in disdain.

'Stop it now and have some fun and please don't order a cosmopolitan here. Have the same as me, it's manlier for you,' I whisper back.

'Vodka tonics coming right up. Rajesh? What would you like?' asks Vick. I shut my eyes in fear of the cosmopolitan.

'Uh, okay, I'll have the same,' he mumbles.

As we take our first sips, Lara arrives giggling.

I ask, 'What happened?'

'I just saw Reema trip over a wet spot and her two bimbo sidekicks, Reshma and Mona, are trying to pick her up. The entire staff is helping but she is just too heavy!' Lara laughs loudly.

'Oh God, Reema's here?'

Sanya adds, 'I think they might bring a wheelchair for her. She's yelling at the top of her voice.' She nods towards their direction and we all burst out laughing.

Watching a heavy Reema lying prostrate over a puddle with Reshma and Mona trying to lift her up from each side proves to be extremely comical and gives us a bout of sadistic pleasure watching her in pain.

Reshma is Reema's dumb sidekick. More than being dumb she is blank. At least Mona smiles stupidly; Reshma chooses to stare into empty space. Despite seeming naive and blank, she is known to be quite the man-stealer. She is considered the biggest 'sucker' (pun intended) in town, leaching into anything that fancies her; the very reason why I intend to keep her away from Rajesh. Although, I doubt Rajesh would be lured into her trap that easily: she doesn't have long hair, nor is she fair!

Mona, a fair and slightly-on-the-plump-side girl, is the nicest in comparison to the other two, perhaps because she is the dumbest too. Mona apparently never actually graduated from any college, despite spending over five years in various cities across the world! She also has a freaky obsession with Ishaan, forcing him to sprint at the mere sight of her.

Lara laughs, 'Ishaan, time for you to hide! Mona is here!' Ishaan's eyes flash with fright and disgust as he turns his back to their direction.

I glance over at Rajesh to see if he's okay and I find him conversing with the guys. I grab the girls and push them out of Rajesh's earshot.

'So, what do you think?' I ask earnestly.

'Oh, he's nice so far. You guys look pretty good together,' coos Lara.

Sanya adds, 'He doesn't look like a frog, Neha.' I raise my eyebrow at her. 'Okay, fine, maybe a little,' Sanya laughs with the others. I take another large gulp of my drink.

Palak asks, 'What was he whispering to you about? Is he mad about something?'

'No, no,' I lie. 'He was just whispering something else,' I cover up. 'He doesn't like to party too much. He is a lot more sophisticated, you see!' I tease.

'Ohhh . . .' the girls burst out laughing louder.

'I wonder what he's talking to the guys about,' I ponder. 'And how come Ishaan is alone? Where is his model?'

'Uh, hold on, here she comes!' Sanya nudges me and points towards the entrance.

A beautiful, tall and dusky woman walks in. Or shall I say girl? Large smouldering eyes, a sensual pout, and a super tiny skirt teamed with a tight graphic T-shirt, a few layers of make-up and loose wavy hair falling to her shoulders. Every man at Aer turns to ogle at her. She walks straight towards Ishaan where he is trying to convince a reluctant Rajesh to have another shot. The model carelessly steps in between Rajesh the toad and handsome Ishaan, places her hand around Ishaan's waist and smiles seductively. Ishaan forgets all about Rajesh and hands her the shot glass instead. They both down the shot and the model giggles flirtatiously while caressing his chest.

The other guys simply stare and humbly sip their drinks. Rajesh gapes foolishly at the model, who is at least 5 inches taller than him even in her flat ballerinas. Palak, Lara and I quickly go to our men's side while Sanya walks up to Ishaan to get introduced to his latest squeeze.

'Rajesh, why don't you and I take a shot together?' I smile widely, trying to tear his eyes away from the gorgeous dusky goddess.

'You're done with your drink?' he exclaims and then he rolls his eyes, 'Fine, just one.'

So much for trying!

I ask for two shots of kamikazes and as I am about to toast with him, I decide to talk to him first.

I move closer and ask, 'Rajesh, tell me honestly, what is going on? Why are you so annoyed? Can you at least smile, lighten up and enjoy the evening with me?'

Rajesh places his arms around my waist and pulls me closer, 'Of course I want to enjoy it with you, but I want to spend time with you alone, not with everyone else. Even models!'

Why is he being so difficult?

I look over his shoulder at Ishaan and his date. Ishaan is whispering something in her ears. He catches my eye and winks. I return his gesture with a small smile and a half nod, too sad to care. He frowns and raises his eyebrows as if to ask, 'What's wrong'. I shake my head and look back at Rajesh.

Rajesh traces my left cheek with his fingers and then frowns, 'You have a lot of blush on!'

That's it.

I take a deep breath and bite my lower lip in order to stop myself from saying anything too nasty.

My decision is made.

'Sorry,' I reply tightly.

He frowns, 'Don't be too sad, it's okay, there is a next time. Come on, drink up.'

At least he notices my mood!

I chug the shot, not tasting the alcohol.

Rajesh leans and kisses me with his wet lips and then rubs the small of my back. 'I still like you, don't take everything so seriously, Neha.'

'Hmm . . .' I murmur, and look around for the others.

Does he not realize anything? Is he that stupid?

I feel tears welling up in my eyes and I try blinking them away.

Time to let him go.

The others return in a good mood; clearly they had been having more fun shots than Rajesh and I.

Sanya gushes, 'Look at you two, sharing a romantic moment together!'

If she only knew.

'Guys, I think we need to take a break!' exclaims a drunk Lara.

I get myself another vodka tonic and finish off half my drink, blatantly ignoring Rajesh's frog stares. In the meantime, the guys gather and take more drinks together, laughing and slapping each other's backs.

'I think it's gonna be a good night after all,' smiles Lara, dreamily glancing at Ashish.

She really is drunk!

'I think we drank too much, too fast!' she giggles.

'I think it's not enough!' says Palak quietly. She glances at Raj and then looks away without a smile. She takes my drink and chugs it.

'What's wrong?' I frown. Palak would never say something like this.

Maybe she had a little fight with Raj.

'Nothing. One more shot!' she shouts.

'No! Enough!' Sanya exclaims. 'You all have guys to go home with, I'm going home alone,' she whines. 'My guy is spending quality time with his family.' She rolls her eyes.

We stop and stare at her.

'What?' I ask stunned.

'Oh nothing, I'm just rambling! Shot, shot, shot! Come on!' she laughs as she walks back to the bar.

I look at the other two to discuss what Sanya just said, but

Lara is staring dreamily at Ashish and Palak is in her own world, trying not to stare at Raj. I assemble them at the bar.

The guys see the deadly shots Sanya has arranged for us and insist on joining us.

Sanya laughs back, 'Sorry boys, this one is only for the ladies!'

Rajesh suddenly appears amidst the bigger built guys, his eyes popping out wider. 'Another shot? What the fuck!' He comes towards me in shock, 'Neha?'

Vick shouts from the back, 'Relax, Rajesh, these girls can really handle their spirits!' Rajesh grunts and I purposely ignore his words.

'To us girls, for always being absolutely fabulous!'

'This shot is disgusting! Sanya! What the hell is this shit?' I yell.

Sanya laughs, 'It's time for tonight's black out!' she giggles.

When I turn around, all I can see are Rajesh's large eyes. 'Can I get you some water?'

'No! I want another vodka tonic with a slice of lime,' I insist stubbornly.

'No, how about something more sophisticated? Like some wine. Red or white?' Rajesh insists.

'Mmm . . . fine, white,' I answer.

'Okay.'

I stand next to him at the bar as the bartender brings out three different bottles, the labels of which are all blurry to me. As I half hear him discuss the contents of each bottle with the bartender, I catch him ask loudly the worst question possible in the world of chivalry:

'How much is each glass?'

'Rs 850 for this, Rs 950 for this one and Rs 1200 for this one, sir.'

'Okay, give me that one.'

I freeze.

Sanya and Lara stop talking nearby and stare.

They heard it!

I avoid their stares and continue looking down.

I hear Sanya whisper, 'Did he just ask the price of a *glass* of wine? For his date?'

Rajesh, hands me the glass and I say a meek thanks.

I cannot believe he did this!

'Rajesh do you want to go home?' I ask.

'Oh of course, whenever you want to go. Finish up your wine and we'll leave.'

I finish it in less than fifteen minutes and turn to him to leave.

I say my goodbyes to my drunken friends, who hug and kiss me over a hundred times.

When I go up to Ishaan, he hugs me tightly and whispers, 'I hope everything is okay? Call me if you need anything.' He smiles warmly at me and winks as I withdraw from his arms. The hot model stares daggers at me and I quickly leave in fear of being trampled on.

With my vision and other senses slightly blurred on the drive back I hear, 'I don't like Ishaan. Why does he date models only? And why does he have to kiss you?'

'Huh?' I ask confused. 'Why does it bother you?'

'Well, he seems quite shallow.'

I ignore him, preferring to close my eyes.

'And is Sanya with someone?'

'What?'

'Is she dating anyone?'

'No.'

Rajesh smirks and shakes his head.

What is his issue in life?

I get angry, 'Why do you not like my friends?'

'It's not that I don't like them; I am just wondering how you get along with all of them! They're just party animals!'

'Why are you so judgemental? You need to loosen up a bit. They are just normal people. Maybe you have grown too old! You don't like girls if they have short hair or enjoy a laugh here and there. What is the matter with you?'

'Oh please, Natasha has nothing to do with this,' he says defensively.

'Whatever!' I retort, not interested in continuing the conversation.

But he drones on, lecturing me on the vices of drinking so much and on social etiquette and why there shouldn't be more guys than girls around me.

By the time we reach my building, I resist even before he can make a suggestion, 'No need to come with me, I can go up on my own.'

I see him through blurry vision. 'You drink too much, Neha,' I hear him say and then feel a brush on my lips.

At least I get a goodnight kiss!

EXPECT THE UNEXPECTED

'*I gotta feeling . . . tonight's . . .*'

'Hi baby,' Rajesh greets me brightly.

'Mmm . . . Good morning. It's Sunday, why are you awake?' I lazily stretch out, checking the time; it's only 10.15.

'I was thinking of you.'

'What? Why?' I ask confused.

'Neha, I'm crazy about you.'

'What? It's still morning,' I grumble.

'Oh my God, you are so insensitive, Neha,' he sounds angry.

'I'm sorry, Rajesh. It's just that it's morning and I have to get ready soon for a champagne brunch with the girls.'

'What? You girls are going to drink again?'

'Rajesh! What is your problem? It is just brunch. It's not like we are doing anything stupid.'

Okay, we all do get really wasted quite often, but come on, it's all in good spirit. I mean it is 2011 after all. The world is going to end in 2012 so we might as well live it up till then.

'No Neha, it's not good for you. You are twenty-five. You need to start behaving responsibly now, especially when you want to get married. What if you start behaving like this even after marriage?'

Are you seriously kidding me?

'Rajesh, you need to relax and stop lecturing. I am going out with my friends to eat food. I don't want to hear a lecture from you in the morning,' I lose my cool.

Silence.

'Neha, we can discuss this nicely. You don't need to shout.'

'What is there to discuss? And by the way, Rajesh, you don't discuss. You preach.'

'Please stop behaving like this. Are you really always this strong-headed? Are you always going to want it your way?'

'Rajesh, I have to go get ready. We'll talk later.' I hang up.

Wow. Our first fight. But how dare he lecture me like this. And call me irresponsible. Jackass. I need to break up with him soon.

I try to push him out of my mind as I storm into the shower.

Good morning Neha!

Y

Our brunch meets always make for an eventful Sunday filled with mimosas and bellinis and especially so when we visit our usual Sunday brunch joint—Olive. It serves fabulous fare—a variety of delicacies and more importantly, unlimited booze. There is practically no better way for a group of girls to unwind after a hectic week and bitch about all the men and mothers in their lives. We make it a point to wear tights below our skirts as the free-flowing champagne generally leads at least one of us to miss a step or two. Our brunch sessions usually end with us stumbling out of the restaurant and rushing home for a perfectly sound snooze, in other words, to pass out in peace.

Lara, Palak and I settle down at our table with mimosas and salads. As usual, Sanya arrives fashionably late in one of her usual daring outfits: micro mini denim skirt and a chest-hugging white strapless top, four-and-a-half-inch red Manolo Blahniks, and oversized Chanel sunglasses. She sits down, indifferent to the attention she gets at every step, and rummages through her large Prada bag, taking out her BlackBerry first, then her wallet, a candy bar, mints, and then finally a sealed envelope. Leaving the other items on the table, she removes four pink coloured passes from the envelope.

As she holds out the passes delicately with her manicured nails, she announces proudly, 'These are passes for tomorrow night's fashion show in which every hot eligible bachelor is going to be present!'

Lara retorts, 'No, there will be no hotties, just gays and asexual types. Oh and a few perverts.'

'Fashion show?' inquires Palak hesitantly, looking towards me across the table. We all exchange worried glances at each other. The last time Sanya got herself involved in a fashion show, she came out of it with a male model who, we were convinced, was a either a bisexual or a professional gigolo looking for his next meal!

'Come on guys, it's for a good cause. And we are going to have loads of fun, plus there is free-flowing wine and champagne. My NGO has tied up with the event along with my friend, Sanjay's company.'

'Mmm . . .' I ponder as I play with my asparagus salad, 'Is Sanjay by any chance the *family* guy you were talking about on Friday night?'

Sanya shifts uncomfortably. 'Erm . . . Okay, so are you guys coming or not?' she ignores my question.

I glance at Palak, but she seems to be in her own world. Her eyes appear small behind her glasses.

'Yes, yes, count me in,' Lara grins as she pops a baby tomato into her mouth.

'Neha,' Sanya directs her stare at me, 'Come on, forget about Rajesh, he can't start influencing your decisions already!'

My mind wanders to the morning's conversation with Rajesh. He really is showing his true colours, which are shades of grey. We haven't even come close to making a decision on marriage, well at least I haven't, and he is becoming possessive about me. Even speculating on how I will behave after marriage. Talk about jumping to conclusions. He dislikes my friends even before getting to know them properly, and has an issue with me going out anywhere!

Who cares, I am breaking up with him anyways.

'Fine, I'm coming,' I reply and with that I become the first to finish my mimosa.

'Sooo . . . tell us about Rajesh!' coos Sanya. 'Do you want to know what we think about him?'

'Do I really want to know?' I raise an eyebrow. The three giggle. 'Do you want to know what he thinks about you guys?'

'What?' asks Lara.

'Of course he loved us and found us truly fascinating!' declares Sanya confidently.

'Oh yes, fascinating indeed!' I laugh.

'So considering you have been with him for so long, is there a possibility that you're going to be getting married soon?'

'Shut up! First you have to tell us, who is this family guy you've been talking about?' I ask back.

'Yeah, I am curious too. You were acting so strange at Aer—what have you been up to?' asks Lara.

'Do you even remember anything from that night, Lara?' Sanya retorts.

'Sanjay?' I ask pointedly.

'No, I told you we are just friends and I'm not doing anything with him,' insists Sanya.

'Are you falling for him?' I ask innocently.

'No, I am not,' she replies heatedly.

'Okay, okay, relax! I'm just asking,' I slur. The champagne cocktails are starting to do their job well.

'Oh, by the way, I keep forgetting to tell you guys. Rita asked me to apply for a promotion to be an assistant to the account executive for Harry's account. She is going to keep a closer eye on my work and decide soon.'

'Wow! What did you say?'

'I just said okay,' I shrug.

'This is big! Why didn't you say something before?' asks Sanya.

'It is?'

'Yes! Oh my God, Neha! You are finally moving up from being a trainee for like three years!' exclaims Lara.

'I really don't care. I am happy where I am. I don't need it. Plus, it will be so much more responsibility.'

Lara frowns at me, 'Neha, are you serious? Can you hear yourself?'

Uh oh! Lecture time!

'Palak, why are you so quiet?' I try moving the conversation away from my issues. And wondering why Palak hasn't reacted yet about my job dilemma.

'Oh nothing, just sleepy,' Palak answers softly. 'Can I have one more bellini?'

Lara picks on her grilled prawns vigorously and asks, 'What colour should Ashish's sherwani be?'

Palak gently tugs on her necklace and absentmindedly says, 'White with gold embroidery.'

'Okay, why is everyone in their own daze today? Come on, drink more,' I get annoyed.

Brunch is not supposed to this quiet. Where have all our famous toasts gone? Why has everyone become serious all of a sudden?

Beep. BBM from Rajesh: 'Please don't drink too much. Come see me after ;)'

Yeah, right. I am going to sleep after this, especially since the bastard woke me up early just because he is crazy about me! What a load of crap.

'Make it two bellinis,' I call out to the waiter.

Lara begins her whining, 'Ashish's sisters want to wear matching outfits. Why the hell would you want to do that? And then the mother! Oh God, now she wants all three of them to wear the same colour. How stupid is that going to look? I hate the whole matching shit. I mean it looks cute on little kids maybe, but not when you are past your puberty and especially not for an important event. I don't understand why they don't think. God has given you a brain so bloody well use it!'

'What colour do they want?' I giggle.

'An ugly brown! I tried suggesting other colours but they refuse to take my advice.'

'Oh God, it's the three bitches,' whispers Palak.

Lara rolls her eyes and says, 'Ugh, not right now, it's still friggin' morning; too early for me to deal with these fat asses.'

Sanya puts on her socialite smile and turns around to wave at Reema, Mona and Reshma.

'No, Sanya,' I grumble defeated.

The three bitches struggle to get through the entrance since their extra large hips require double doors. Once through, as if on cue, they lift their oversized sunglasses to their heads and start scanning the restaurant. Their matching frilly, multi-coloured dresses make their butts look even bigger. They always make it a point to wear clothes, bags and shoes of high-end designers and flaunt price tags all the while cribbing about how expensive things are. They catch sight of us and adjust their bags to ensure their designer logos are strategically placed for visual effect and walk towards us. I shift uncomfortably in my seat, praying that Reema doesn't bring up Rajesh's topic.

Reema eyes me suspiciously and even before exchanging pleasantries, drops the bombshell, 'So how do you know Rajesh?' She asks in her trademark derogatory tone.

Shit.

Reshma and Mona join Reema and start checking out the others, invariably trying to calculate the cost of each outfit and bag. They would have wanted to see the shoes too, but for that they'd have to bend down and that would take too much effort, besides flashing the others with an unpleasant sight of their backsides.

'Where's Ishaan these days?' asks Mona. We refuse to reply. Ishaan had done a good job hiding from her at Aer.

Reema struggles with her large Balenciaga as she lays it on our table with a thud and looks towards Lara. 'See, I bought this from my recent trip to Milan, and I loved it so much that I bought it in green as well as blue. I saw the small one you have there too, but I liked this much more.'

Lara retorts, 'Oh, of course, the bigger size suits your frame too.'

Reema for some reason is always picking on Lara and we have unanimously decided that she is simply jealous of Lara's engagement to Ashish. Luckily, Lara doesn't have to worry much since Reema is universally hated.

But one thing is for sure, we always dread the presence of the deadly threesome because of their professional gossiping skills, spreading rumours like wildfire, rumours that have that deathly possibility of ruining you. Everyone fears them, except Lara of course! She fears nobody.

Reema conveniently ignores Lara's comment and looks

at her next *bakra*—Palak. 'So I heard about Hong Kong, congratulations!'

Lara, Sanya and I exchange confused and bewildered glances. Sanya blurts out, 'What?'

Palak squirms in her chair and looks very uncomfortable. She nods curtly and gives a tight, 'Thanks.'

Reema notices the change in atmosphere and doesn't miss the opportunity, 'What? You haven't yet told your friends the good news? Palak is going to move to Hong Kong!' She snorts, 'Some friendship you lot have!'

She smiles smugly at having done her bad deed for the day, lifts her bright green Balenciaga and starts walking away, followed by her dumb and dumber entourage. It's certain she is going to digest her food well today.

She finds it difficult to manoeuvre between the tables with her nose up in the air and her massive bottom knocks over a wine glass. The other two are more careful, afraid to disturb any more glassware.

With the amount of champagne in my system I normally would have laughed my ass off, but I was still stunned about Reema's news about Palak.

Palak is moving? Have I been so wound up in my own life that I never ask Palak about her life? But still, how can she not tell us?

Sanya breaks the stunned silence and asks, 'Palak, what's going on?'

Palak sits there with a glum look and breaks the news to us. 'I got promoted and that requires me to go to Hong Kong.'

'For how long?'

'Forever.'

'And Raj?'

'I don't know. I mean he hasn't proposed, he hasn't even said anything like "please don't go". He hasn't even said "let's get engaged". And I really, really want to go to Hong Kong. It's a big achievement, especially for a woman. Am I supposed to reject the offer just because of my boyfriend? Who hasn't yet talked about a future together?'

'Wait, so what did Raj say?'

'Well, he hasn't said anything yet. I just found out two days ago and I have no idea how Reema knows! When I called Raj to tell him, he just said, "Wow, congratulations, I'm so proud of you my love." I didn't know what he was implying, so I just said thanks. It's like last month we were so steady and serious, and now we are one of those casual couples who stay together if it suits them and breaks up at any inconvenience.'

'Did you tell him, as in specify, that you had to move?'

'Yes I did, twice, and he didn't respond at all,' she replies sombrely.

'Nothing?' asks an astonished Lara.

'Yes, yes, nothing! It's like he just doesn't care. In short, I have wasted the last four years of my life on an idiot who doesn't even care about me or that I am moving to a whole new country!' Palak's eyes start to well up with tears.

Oh my God, how can this happen to Palak and Raj? They are the only ones we know that are a 'normal' couple.

'Last night I called and asked him if it was okay with him if I move to Hong Kong and we do long distance, and he replied angrily that there is no point in continuing long distance and that we might as well break up, and so I replied, "Yes we should break up then," and I hung up. I haven't spoken to him since. So yeah, we've broken up now.'

We sit there in staggering silence, still trying to recuperate from the blow. First, Palak leaving us and second, her break up.

'Don't you think you're overreacting a bit? Shouldn't you at least hear Raj out?' asks Sanya quietly.

'Hear what? He has not said anything about it since I told him, so he clearly has nothing to say. I mean nothing to him. He didn't even ask "what about us?" and at Aer he acted totally normal as if nothing had happened.'

'Oh my God, Palak, why didn't you say anything to us? Has he called back?' I ask hopefully.

'A few times, but I am not picking up. I have too much to figure out before I leave.'

'Is that why you were all weird on Friday with him? Wait, you're leaving? For real?'

'Yes,' Palak replies forcefully.

'When?' I panic.

'In a month maybe. I have two weeks to give my final decision.'

'What do you really want to do, Palak?' probes Lara gently.

'Honestly, I don't know. I mean, I worked so hard and I really deserve this position, and I want to do this for myself, but I also love Raj and I can't think of my life without him. But he hasn't said anything about us or our future. And the way he reacted clearly gives me my answer, that there is no use waiting around here for him to propose; that way I will lose out both ways. Raj took me for granted. He thinks I can just hang around for him without ever pressuring him into anything or nagging him about marriage,' she speaks rapidly. 'And I don't want to force him into marrying me; he should want to do it on his own. Plus in Hong Kong I can start a new life, away from my past. I just feel so hurt and stupid. The least Raj can do is talk to me about what is on his mind,' her voice breaks. 'Even if it is something like "I want to break up".' Palak takes a sharp breath, 'I don't understand him any more.'

'Just give it some time Palak. It is probably just as overwhelming for him,' Lara explains.

'I don't know what to do.'

'I think you should call him ASAP and hear him out. Or better, meet him.'

'Hmm . . .' she murmurs as she finishes off another bellini.

'All right, maybe we should go home and Palak you should go see Raj now,' instructs Lara.

Sanya starts fiddling with her phone. 'Yeah, I agree.'

'Okay, but after one last drink. Sanya get off your phone. And Palak, call us after and we can come over.'

After the last drops of the bellinis are drunk in a depressed and sombre mood with Palak still sniffling, we get up to leave.

'Sanya, are you coming with me?' I ask.

'Uh, no, I'm gonna finish off an errand first,' she replies.

Lara and I frown at each other but realize our attention needs to be on Palak right now.

For the first time we all remember leaving brunch.

LOVE BEGINS WITH A SMILE, GROWS WITH A KISS AND ENDS WITH A TEARDROP

Palak calls weeping.

'The bastard says he's not ready to get engaged yet and that he needs time,' she sobs. 'Is four years not good enough? How much time does he need? A hundred years?' Palak cries out aloud, 'And before he could say or justify any of the shit he was saying, I just yelled at him, "Don't bother, I am not interested in someone as flaky as you any more," and I stormed out of his house.' Through uncontrollable wailing she stutters, 'It's over. It's all over now.'

'Oh no, I am coming over now. Have you reached home?'

'Yes,' she cries.

I dial Lara's number, 'Palak is howling, I am going over to her place, wanna come?'

'Okay, yeah, I'll see you there.'

I call Sanya but she doesn't pick up. I send her a BBM: 'Call ASAP. We are going to Palak's place, meet us there.'

Sanya returns my call as I get into my building lift.

'Where are you?' I ask.

'Uh, what happened?' she ignores my question.

'Palak's bawling her eyes out. Raj clearly didn't say anything right.'

'Okay, I'll see you there,' she hangs up immediately.

Where does this girl disappear all the time?

As I enter Palak's flat I find her mother standing outside Palak's bedroom, knocking on her door. Her face is stricken with worry.

'Palak beta, please open the door,' her mother cries out. She turns towards me and anxiously asks, 'Neha, what's going on?'

Oh crap. What am I supposed to say?

'Aunty, don't worry, she will be fine. Let me talk to her,' I clasp her mother's shoulders.

'Neha, what happened to her? I have never seen her like this,' she asks worried.

'Palak, it's me, Neha, open the door,' I call out while tapping her door. I hear something smash on the ground.

Shit, this doesn't sound good.

I turn to Palak's mother, 'Aunty, let me handle this. Lara and Sanya are on their way. Don't worry, she will be fine.' I try to put on a reassuring smile.

She nods in resignation and walks away towards her own room.

'Please call me if you need anything,' she says. I nod.

The door unlocks and I am faced with a swollen-eyed, red-faced and dishevelled Palak, in shabby grey sweatpants and a messy ponytail with her glasses perched on top of her head.

'That bastard!' she yells and then falls into my arms and sobs uncontrollably.

'Shh, it's okay, sit down.' I caress her head, 'The others are coming. Here, I got you some candy, chocolate ice cream and chips.'

As I lead her back into her room by the shoulders, I see photo frames with pictures of Raj and her flung across the floor, two shoe boxes covered with pink wrapping paper thrown open with its contents spilling out on the floor. The love boxes as she calls them are where she keeps every small memory of Raj over the past four years; photographs, letters, cards, ribbons, dried flowers and other kinds of trinkets.

I guide Palak carefully over the strewn items towards the bed. She plops face down and howls even more.

'I hate him. I hate him. I hate him. I hate him,' she rants on from under the covers.

'We hate him too,' announces Lara as she enters into the room with a bag full of comfort food.

'Why do we always pig out when it comes to boys?' I groan as I make an unsuccessful attempt at trying to resist reaching for a bag of chips from Lara.

Five minutes later, a flustered Sanya rushes into the bedroom and plonks down on the bed next to Palak.

'What happened to you?' scorns Lara, eyeing Sanya's crumpled top, the same one she was wearing for our brunch, and messy hair.

'I was yelling after you to ask you to wait for me by the lift and you made me run!' grumbles a dishevelled Sanya.

'Pull your top up at least!' Lara points out. Sanya struggles to keep her voluptuousness inside her strapless top.

'Sanya, you ran? Wow! You never run!' I ask surprised.

'Oh shut up,' and Sanya nods towards Palak, still lying on her stomach and cradling her head between her arms.

'Palak, tell us what happened.'

'Ice cream first,' she sobs.

'Here,' I lift open the lid of the ice cream tub and give everyone plastic spoons.

Palak slowly gets up, grabs the tub and takes two spoonfuls, allowing the ice cream to melt slowly in her mouth.

'Oh, hurry up and gulp it. We want to know what happened,' says an impatient Sanya.

'Mmm,' Palak murmurs as she swallows the chocolate ice cream. 'He is a bastard. They're all fucking bastards,' she fumes.

'Do you wanna expand on that?' I ask.

'Well I went over to his place like you told me to. Raj was lounging in his stupid boxers, drinking a beer and watching TV. Completely relaxed! When he saw me, he just smiled and said, "Hi." No remorse, none of the "Oh I missed you" shit. As soon as I heard that, I got so pissed off I wanted to break the fucking beer bottle over his head. I mean seriously, after something this big, who the fuck just says, "Hi"?' she rages.

'Then what happened?'

'So, I took a deep breath and as calmly as I could, I asked "What's going to happen with us?" and he just replied, "What do you mean?" while taking another sip from his beer bottle. He didn't understand me and acted as if everything was normal. So I reminded him that I'll be moving to Hong Kong soon. And he looked so surprised—as if he was hearing it all for the first time. He said, "Wait, are you actually going to accept it?" He had no idea that I was serious about the whole thing! So I tried to remain calm and said, "Why not? It is good for my career." And all that he could think of saying was, "But what will happen to *me*?"' Palak imitates him furiously. 'He said, "You know I love you." So I just bluntly asked him, "So I should leave everything just because you love me?" And for some reason the dimwit thought that I was worried about infidelity and spent half an hour talking about how he never thinks about fucking other girls.'

'So, he really doesn't get it?' I ask bewildered.

'Can you imagine how frustrated I got?' Palak starts crying again. 'So then, I just straightaway asked him if he had any intentions of settling down with me. And he looked so stunned! As if he had seen an alien!' She picks up a small teddy bear from her bed and hurls it across the room in her fury.

'What?' exclaims an appalled Sanya, wolfing down another packet of chips.

'He said, "Of course I do, when *the time is right*!"' Palak raises her hands to do air quotes. 'That's something I have been hearing since a fucking decade now. I mean I thought that this move would at least shake him. But it didn't. And honestly speaking, I don't think he is ever going to be ready and the right fucking time is never going to come for him. I told him that I am ready for marriage and if he is not then we should just call it off. If I know that I don't have a future with him and still stay back I would be seriously compromising my career. Then he started shouting at the top of his voice saying he isn't ready for marriage and that he loves me and only me and it's just a "matter of time". So I started yelling back.'

'In his house?' asks Lara with astonishment, her mouth full of candy.

'Where else?' Tears drop incessantly from Palak's eyes. 'I basically said that if you love me and don't want anyone else, what is so *not* right about the time now? He started to stomp about and said, "What the fuck is the big deal about marriage, it's just a fucking piece of paper and there is no meaning to it. Where is this marriage idea even coming from?" For God's sake, we both are already twenty-six years old and we have been together since forever,' she says, frustrated. 'I continued shouting and swearing my ass off and stormed out.' She pauses, 'That's when I saw his parents standing outside the room. They had heard my howling and even my swearing! When I opened the door to leave, I even yelled back,' she gets animated and her pitch rises. '"Don't you dare call me ever again you bastard because I hate you and I don't even want to marry you any more! You're a fucking coward. And I want a man with balls and I want to have smart kids with brains. And if I marry you, my children would end up with rocks in their heads."'

Palak suddenly cracks up while the three of us gasp and stare at her in shock.

'They heard every word,' she adds. 'His parents sure never imagined this side of me!' Palak grins mischievously.

We all burst out laughing, visualizing little-miss-well-behaved shouting, yelling and swearing in front of elders, especially Raj's parents!

'But Palak, what does your gut say? I mean you do have every reason to react like this, but do you not want to wait?' asks Lara, the hopeful romantic.

'No way,' Palak answers firmly. 'I'm really, really angry. I am so angry that if Raj were here right now, I would definitely shove that beer bottle so high up his ass that he'd be shitting for the rest of his life,' she says with a straight face while the rest of us are in splits.

'You know what, I will be okay,' Palak says as she wipes away her tears, sniffling her red nose.

'Of course you will, don't worry. Just give it some time,' Lara pats her arm.

A visibly upset Sanya takes the chocolate ice cream and starts digging in. 'This is so horrible,' she crinkles up her eyes with a sad face.

'What is wrong with you? It's Palak's break up,' I narrow my eyes.

'Nothing. Stop picking on me Neha,' Sanya whines. 'I am just thinking, how can this happen with Palak and Raj?'

'Hmm . . . that's true. It makes us all sad,'

'Are there no normal guys out there who we can trust? Am I going to remain single for the rest of my life?'

'Hey, it's my crying day, not yours. You're in fact lucky you don't have to deal with any of this fucking relationship shit,' says Palak.

'Oye! Stop swearing like a truck driver, Palak!' shouts Lara to which Palak replies with a dirty look.

Sanya gives a shrug and continues delving into the ice cream tub. I join in.

'I am going to have to start packing soon,' comments Palak.

'Palak! No!' I screech.

'Yes. I have made up my mind,' she responds determinedly.

'No, I think you need to sleep over it. Make your decision when your mind is calm.'

'My decision is made,' she declares stubbornly. 'And I doubt I am going to have a calm mind for a while now.'

'How long do you have to make your final decision?'

'Two weeks.'

'Okay, so inform them on the last day,' I state.

She frowns indignantly.

'Palak, promise me.'

'Fine. But I am still going to start packing because I am definitely going.'

'Okay, fine, if that is what you want, we support you.'

Palak suddenly gets up from the bed and opens her cupboard. She takes out a carefully wrapped box from the top shelf and throws it aggressively on the bed.

'Lara, you take this, shred it into bits and pieces and feed it to the dogs.'

'What is it?'

Lara opens the box and inside lies a beautiful purple lehenga, embroidered and studded with Swarovski crystals. The blouse is a sexy bustier with intricate embroidery and diamond-studded straps and the dupatta is a gorgeous diamond-accentuated accessory.

'I had imagined our engagement to have a purple-and-gold theme with purple and white orchids everywhere. A huge, white cake with purple flowers and lots and lots of champagne and strawberries. And Etta James playing our song *At Last.*'

'Oh wow! This is absolutely stunning! Palak, when did you buy this?' exclaims Lara, fingering the thread work on the lehenga.

'A few months back. I saw it and fell in love with it and thought I would wear it on my engagement day with Raj,' she says bitterly.

'Oh my God! Is it a Tarun Tahiliani?'

'Yep!'

'No way! No fucking way are you going to throw this! I will not let you!' declares Sanya.

'When I saw it, I only had Raj in mind. I don't even want to look at it any more.'

'You can wear it to Lara's wedding,' I suggest. 'You can't waste it like that.'

To which Palak throws me a dirty look.

'Sorry,' I mumble back.

'I just want it out of my house.'

'Okay, okay, fine. I will take it. But I am not throwing it away. Neha is right; you will wear it to my wedding,' instructs Lara firmly.

'Whatever, I just want it out of my sight right now.'

We sit in silence as we dig further into the chips and ice cream.

'Etta James? Really?' I ask out of the blue to which Lara punches me in the arm.

'I can't believe it's over,' Palak says softly.

'Aw, come here,' Lara moves over to hug her.

'Neither can I,' says Sanya quietly as she zones out and eats another spoon of ice cream.

'Sanya?'

'Huh?' she snaps out of her zone.

'What's going on with you?' I narrow my eyes.

'Nothing. I'm sad with all the break ups going on.'

'What break ups? It's only Palak,' I raise my eyebrow.

I hadn't mentioned anything about my intentions with Rajesh.

'Yes, but you know what I mean. I don't like break ups. Especially when it happens to one of us.'

'Hello! I'm right here,' Palak says indignantly.

'I know, I'm sorry, but it is true. I, in fact, *we*, never thought this would happen to you.'

I frown at Sanya, 'What is really going on with you? Your break ups are never sad!'

In fact, Sanya's break ups lead to happier times. On the night of the split, she goes out partying, takes a million shots, dances like crazy and the next day her life goes back to normal, as if nothing had happened. Her recovery period never lasts longer than five hours. But then again, Sanya never really falls in love. The men fall in love with her. She really just wants to have fun with the men she dates. She has yet to meet the one who can really sweep her off her feet.

'Screw you!' Sanya grumbles and lifts her middle finger at me as she eats another spoonful of ice cream.

'Okay fine, sorry, I won't pick on you,' I roll my eyes.

'I think you should go talk to your mother. She's really worried,' says Lara.

'Yeah, I will now. I think she is going to be even more heartbroken than me,' Palak laughs bitterly. 'It's a pity there are no guarantees in life. Makes it all the more fucked up.'

'Well, if it makes you feel any better, I'm planning to break it off with Rajesh.'

'What?' Palak's eyes fly open. 'Why?'

'Neha, are you serious?' asks a shocked Lara.

'Well, I'm not happy; I just don't feel any chemistry at all, despite trying really hard. And he seems to have a problem with everything about me.'

The three of them look at each other for what seems like a millennium.

'Well, are you okay?' asks Sanya finally.

'Yes actually, I feel fine. I'm planning to tell him soon.'

'Really?' asks Lara.

'Yep,' I nod.

'Oh, thank God!' bursts out Sanya while Palak and Lara join in the laughter.

I look at them in shock, wondering where this reaction was coming from.

'Come on, Neha, we knew this was going to happen sooner or later. Plus we didn't really like him. He was so snooty, like he thought he was above us. Who does he think he is anyway?' says an annoyed Lara.

'I know your parents are concerned but don't worry, you'll find someone better than him for sure!' says Sanya. 'Okay, so now dish it, did you sleep with him?'

'No!'

'Are you serious?'

'Yes.'

'How did he kiss?'

'Just fine, thank you very much,' I reply heatedly.

'Hmm . . . stop blushing,' Sanya laughs even harder.

'Have you told your parents yet that you want to dump him?' asks Palak.

'I am not dumping him. I don't like that word, don't use it. I'm just gently saying goodbye to him,' I insist.

'Aww, you're going to break the little frog's heart! If he has one that is!' laughs Sanya.

'This is great! All the guys are breaking hearts; finally a girl is going to break a guy's heart. But who would have thought that Neha would be the one!' Sanya squeals, holding her sides.

'Oye, what does that mean? I can break hearts if I want to.'

'And of all the men in the world, Neha is going to break that arrogant frog's heart!' Lara has tears rolling down her cheeks from laughing so hard.

'Wow, you guys really didn't like him!'

'No!' Lara laughs, 'Palak, you owe me one thousand rupees!'

'What?' I shriek.

'We had a bet; I said it wouldn't last longer than two months.'

'Oh my God! Lara!' and I look over at Sanya accusingly.

'No, no, I don't bet on such predictable things; I need more challenge,' she smirks.

I throw a pillow at her but can't stop myself from laughing as well. *They are right after all and I have a feeling that my mother is going to react in a similar manner.*

'Do you remember his face when we brought the shots out at Aer? He was like, "What the fuck!"' Lara imitates Rajesh, enlarging her eyes like a frog.

I can't help bursting out laughing. He is such a bore! I recall how he was so angry by the end of that night at Aer and how he ranted on about my friends.

'God, that definitely cheered me up!' says Palak, wiping a tear. I smile, glad to have made her laugh, even if it was at my cost. Or rather, Rajesh's cost.

IN CHARITY THERE ARE NO EXCESSES

This charity fashion event, like any other high-profile do is a typical page *trois soirée*, with a few gays, models, escorts, pimps, the works! Here, marriage is taboo talk; there is no mention of the solitaire wedding ring or something as ghastly as lifelong commitment. The conversations revolve around cocaine, alcohol, the casual hook ups, holidays at exotic locales, where everyone tries to get into (from front or behind!) one another's pants. In short, a great break from the Gujarati social dos.

Tonight's show is a collaboration between budding new designers and the elite personalities affiliated with various well-meaning NGOs.

Lara and I decide to leave together without Palak. Palak is in no mood to see or meet people; Raj had not called again to console her, to apologize, or even to simply 'talk'.

Lara picks me up and the first thing she does as I get into the back seat with her is inspect me from head to toe.

'I knew it, come here,' Lara takes out a blush compact from her tiny purse and applies it to my cheeks, then takes out a strand of pearls from the same minuscule clutch and fastens it around my neck, all the while shaking her head in frustration.

'There, *now* you look fine,' she purses her lips together, creating tiny dimples on both cheeks.

Fine? Just fine?

I glance over her outfit: a banded silk blood-red dress tied around her neck, showing off her naturally sun-kissed shoulders and arms, nude-coloured Manolo Blahniks and a tiny python skin clutch that holds pearl necklaces, blush, lipstick, lip gloss and God knows what else. Massive uncut diamonds and ruby trinkets adorn her ears, a large ruby ring on the right hand and her sparkling four-carat engagement ring on the left. She's sculpted her face beautifully with the nude look and smoky eyes. She is at her *elegantest*, if there is ever such a word! Lara is one of the few who can pull off elegant and sexy together.

No wonder she said that I look just *fine*: I pale in comparison to her in my LBD, plain black heels and a plain black clutch. And my hair is tied back in a ponytail, whilst her thick wavy hair caress her back loosely.

Maybe that's why I am still single; I surround myself with way too many hot friends! Even my mother is considered hotter than me, with all that Botox, caviar facials and other shit that my poor dad pays for unwillingly. He is powerless when it comes to discussions (read: one-sided arguments) regarding how much her appearance costs.

When we finally reach Taj Lands End, the lobby is a chaotic mess as we inch ourselves slowly into the ballroom. While we are searching for Sanya, Lara and I get blocked by a dozen people and we are obliged to stop and exchange friendly, and sometimes fake, gestures, small talk and of course emphasize the *oohs, aahs* and *dah-lings* and yes, the air kisses as well!

By the time we spot Sanya an hour has passed. She is standing with her hands on her hips over some tech guy who is seated at the computer and she does not look very happy. In fact, I have never seen a darker cloud loom over her.

'What's wrong?' I ask immediately.

Despite the angry face, Sanya looks absolutely ravishing in a short golden lamé strapless dress and chunky jewellery accentuating her curves and her translucent skin. Her pouty lips are painted with a faint coral colour, and her kohled eyes set her bare peaches-and-cream complexion aglow, allowing her real beauty to shine through. Her shapely legs are further accentuated by a killer pair of high heels flexing her calf muscles.

'Nothing,' she replies grimly.

She picks up two flutes of champagne from a passing by tray and gulps them down one after the other even before I can reach out for the second glass, thinking it was for me. The tech guy looks down to hide his reddened face.

'Sanya?' asks Lara warningly, 'What is going on? Where is your *friend*?' referring to Sanjay.

'I don't know, and I don't care. He can shack up with his bitch of a wife as much as he wants,' she hisses, her face taut in anger, attracting a few startled stares from people around.

Lara and I exchange worried glances; *where is this coming from and when did it get this far?*

'Sanya, calm down, don't let anyone hear you,' Lara says urgently, pulling her away.

'I am fine,' Sanya retorts, visibly upset and seething with rage.

I look on in shock as her fair skin starts to redden. We had been hoping the rumours were just that, rumours, and nothing more. But it seems like we were doing some wishful thinking.

'Come on, let's take our seats,' Sanya sniffs haughtily and we follow her towards the ramp.

And, of course, like everything else that has to do with Sanya this show is also dramatic: she secures our seats in the third row, directly opposite to the front row seats in which sit Sanjay and his bitch of a wife.

Sanjay is unquestionably a delicious treat to the eyes, fitting the stereotypical corporate big shot to the tee. He is handsome, tall, broad, and looks dapper in a designer suit teamed with his attractive smile and charismatic personality.

His wife, to put it in one word, is *tiny*. She has the most beautiful and expressive eyes, her hair is set high up in an elegant bouffant, with a few tendrils framing her delicate face. Seeing her minuscule frame I have this urgent desire to feed her with fat pieces of juicy steak covered in gorgonzola sauce with a side of cheesy mashed potatoes, followed by a heavenly, decadent double chocolate cake with extra whipped cream! I can't help but stare.

She adorns a Grecian style one-shouldered white dress showing off her bony shoulder and lithe figure—her pink-stained lips smile adoringly at her adulterous husband. Humungous diamonds sparkle brightly against her evenly tanned skin.

She does not even notice us sitting across staring at them; she is too busy greeting, giggling and gossiping with women around her, including Monica the bitch (sans Harry darling). Sanjay sits like an obedient puppy next to her, listening to the ladies.

'She is tiny!' I whisper in amazement.

'Wait till I sit on her,' whispers back Sanya threateningly.

'This is ridiculous Sanya! You really are having an affair with that man? This can get really messy if she finds out,' hisses Lara to Sanya.

'I don't care,' replies Sanya.

'What's her name?' I ask.

'Asha.'

'Sanya! Why didn't you just tell us the truth?' I whisper exasperatedly. 'And that sitting on the other side of her is Monica the bitch, my client!'

'They are like best friends.'

The lights dim and the show begins before we can argue any more.

Sanya continues to stare daggers at the couple until Sanjay catches sight of us. He starts shifting uncomfortably, trying to avoid Sanya's gaze through the passing models strutting in hideous outfits and ornaments more appropriate for clowns.

There clearly is a torrid affair between them. Of all the stupid things Sanya's done, this really takes the cake!

The show ends and everyone mingles around to gush about what a 'great and innovative show that was'! What I thought to be ridiculous, the others found outstanding and a progressive piece of work to give back to the society. I stick to my theory that a bunch of dumb rich people with very little else to do can appreciate anything. Monica passes by me towards Asha, without so much as an acknowledging glance. Sanjay and Asha stick to each other like honeybees, further infuriating Sanya, instigating her to take matters into her hands.

'Watch this,' she informs us.

She daringly catwalks up to a good-looking young man standing nearby, flirtatiously smiles, laughs and links her arm with the surprised man, putting on a wonderful show for Sanjay's benefit. Every few minutes she throws a, 'I don't give a crap about you', glance towards him. As Lara and I look on, there is no mistaking Sanjay turn to the shade of beetroot. His demure wife, however, doesn't seem to notice anything wrong in her husband's demeanour and continues chatting with others. But Monica does.

Monica comes around to Sanjay's side and exchanges a few words with him before pushing him to a corner away from the crowd. They maintain a distance of less than a foot between them and whisper urgently and scandalously into each other's ears. Monica keeps glaring in Sanya's direction and then angrily walks away.

What on earth is going on?

'What the hell is she doing?' whispers Lara under her breath, throwing a dirty look at Sanya who conveniently ignores us.

'He's married! Palak knew something was up,' I respond.

After a while Sanya gets bored with the attention her muse showers her with. She motions us towards the bathroom. Lara lets out a huge sigh of relief as we follow her in.

The bathroom, for a change, is empty and Sanya walks straight to the mirror to admire herself. She frowns in anger as she smoothens her dress, clearly unhappy at what she sees.

'How dare he!' she fumes, placing her two hands on the edge of the counter to hold her trembling body steady.

'Sanya, don't you think you are being a bit unreasonable? He is married for God's sake! Why are you vying for his attention?' Lara shouts at her.

'I don't care. A promise is a promise. Whatever said and done. I don't care any more,' Sanya yells angrily.

'Okay, calm down now,' I say.

Sanya storms into a cubicle and slams the door shut. Lara and I look at each other confused and worried.

Lara shakes her head and motions me to the mirror, opens up her clutch and starts taking out make-up to apply on me.

'Open your purse, let me see what you have,' she orders.

I obediently open up my plain black clutch, which Lara frowns down at disapprovingly.

'We haven't been able to teach you a thing, have we? Just a clear lip gloss? Are you serious?' She looks disgustingly at it as she examines the rest of the contents in my purse.

Lara takes out some rouge to apply on my cheeks, 'I am giving your pale face some colour,' she mutters while we hear the bathroom door open and shut a few times.

A woman stands next to us at the mirror for a while. It takes us some time to realize something seems odd; a tiny little woman with large Cleopatra eyes is staring directly at us in the mirror. It is the bitch of a wife! She stares at us calmly, with complete poise, and then proceeds to apply generous doses of mascara to her eyelashes.

Flush.

Sanya walks out of the cubicle and freezes in her step when she catches sight of Sanjay's wife in the mirror. Asha stops her touch-up job and stares at Sanya through the reflection. Despite her minuscule size, her eyes have a fiery gleam, enough to scare the crap out of me! She is like the green chilli: the tinier they look, the spicier they taste. She turns around calmly and looks Sanya straight in the eye.

Sanya shifts uncomfortably and tries to avert her gaze. Lara and I stop fiddling with the rouge and my mouth falls wide open.

The tiny bitch of a wife blatantly eyes Sanya from top to bottom and smirks loudly, 'So you're the tart,' she says calmly in an amused tone.

So she does know!

I shake my head, worried at how Sanya will rip her apart. Nobody insults Sanya and gets away with it. But Sanya says nothing. Instead she stares at the floor and to my shock, she turns into the colour of Lara's rouge.

In spite of her tiny size in comparison to tall and broad Sanya, Asha is holding her ground strongly and firmly.

'You can dream all you want, but my husband will never leave me and you have no future with him,' Asha speaks softly and casually. 'It's best that you stop now. He is mine and mine only. Now you can run along with your slutty clothes and stay the hell away from me and my husband or else I can assure you I will ruin your life forever.' It sounds like she is having a conversation over cappuccino and crumb cake. But the underlying threat in her voice sends shivers through my spine.

Sanya stands there faltering and shaking; her head bent low in shame. Tears start flowing down and Lara and I rush to her side while the tiny bitch strolls out of the bathroom as if she were in a park. As soon as she exits, a flock of women stumble into the bathroom.

It was a set-up. The tiny bitch had her bitches man the door to prevent anyone from entering while she confronted her husband's mistress.

Bathroom-goers stop and stare at Sanya's tear-streaked face inquisitively. The normal Sanya who can collect herself at any time is nowhere in sight. Her body shakes uncontrollably as tears roll down further. We quickly push her into a cubicle away from prying eyes, seating her down on a covered pot and she starts to howl.

'I really love him, how can this happen to me?' she says in between sobs. She brings up her legs closer to her body, hugging herself in pain. Her mascara smears as tears stream down.

'Sanya, it is okay to let it out,' I say gently, rubbing her arm. Kneeling down beside her in the cramped cubicle clearly not meant for three people is uncomfortable.

But Lara is unable to keep her cool; 'Sanya, I know this is not the time, but what were you thinking? How come you haven't told us anything? You really have been having an affair with a *married* man? You never told us anything! Sanya!'

Sanya shuts her eyes tightly as her face contorts in pain. She shakes her head, 'I know, I'm sorry, I'm sorry, I just couldn't stop myself, and before I knew it I was too in love with him.'

'Does he know you love him?' I probe.

'Yes,' she nods. We look at her questioningly. 'But he . . . he . . .' she struggles, 'he hasn't said anything. He just remains silent. What do I do? I can't ever stop loving him. I love him, I really do. I can't bear to ever live life without him. And I know he loves me too. I know it, he is just too scared to say so,' she insists.

'Shhh . . .' Lara consoles, 'It is okay now; you will be just fine. Let's leave from here, screw these assholes, come on.'

I tear off some toilet paper to wipe Sanya's face and to clean up her spreading kohl.

She sniffs in her last bit of tears and resignedly whispers, 'I wanna go home.'

Lara calls her driver to the front while I help Sanya up. I open the cubicle door first and walk out, holding Sanya's hand. She follows me with her head hung low. The bathroom falls quiet again and everyone stares at us. Lara walks behind, giving dirty looks at the meddlesome crowd. Clearly the word has spread about some kind of showdown with Sanya and it seems like everyone knows details that we don't.

I stick to the walls as I hurry towards the exit to avoid as many people as possible. The people that we do bump into, however, simply stare at Sanya's red and messy-eyed face. An evil, smiling Monica greets us at the exit to ensure we leave.

Is that a victory smile?

Sanjay or his 'bitch of a wife' are nowhere to be seen.

As soon as we are settled into the car, Sanya bursts out howling again.

I have never seen Sanya like this. Sanya never gets hurt, she hurts others; she never cries, she makes others cry. But today is another day altogether. She curls up towards me and bawls like a baby. We reach our building two tissue boxes later, and Lara and I practically carry her up.

When we guide her into her bedroom, we are confronted with a mess: clothes sprawled all over, shoes thrown around and every colour of the rainbow reflecting off her walls. Sanya is still a little girl at heart beneath the exotic and mature looks. Sanya finds her pyjamas, cotton pink ones with Donald Duck on them, and as I help her change, Lara ventures into the kitchen to make some tea.

'Tea?' I had asked horrified. Lara gave me a dirty look and I shut up.

The three of us lay tucked in bed with Sanya sniffling away in the middle, holding a tissue box. She reaches over me to open her side drawer—inside it is a vast assortment of chocolates and candies. She takes out a few boxes, tears them open and starts to attack each one. I help myself to a few Godiva truffles, some Lindt dark chocolate, and some gummy bears and end up with a stomach ache! Sanya keeps going. Lara picks on one truffle for half an hour. As we eat chocolate and sip on tea, we start our bitching session.

'I did not think it would go so far,' says Sanya softly.

'But what gave you the idea that you could get involved with him?'

'I didn't even realize how deeply I fell for him,' she sniffles, her voice choking through tears. 'Before I knew it we were meeting at hotel rooms.' Lara and I exchange surprised glances.

'Oh no, Sanya! Why didn't you tell us?' Lara blurts out.

'Oh my God, so that *was* you who Rajesh and I saw at the Oberoi?' I exclaim.

Sanya burst out howling again, nodding, 'Yes, I am so sorry,' she sobs, 'I hated lying to you. I just didn't know what to do.'

'Shh . . . it's fine now, Sanya, it's over, there is no need to worry,' I console.

'I can't believe that bitch would publicly humiliate me like that. I mean seriously, did she not find any other time? How can she be so . . . so . . .' she struggles for words.

'Such a fucking bitch?' Lara says furiously.

'The whole world must know about it by now. God, I just want to drown in a well,' Sanya says bitterly.

'No way, how will anyone know Sanya?' But while saying so, I look doubtfully at Lara. Lara signals with her eyes to keep shut.

Of course everyone knows by now, and probably knew about the affair way before we did. This is not going to be easy for Sanya. But she doesn't need to think about that now; all she has to do is concentrate on mending her heart and most importantly, stay away from Sanjay.

'I'm ruined now. How am I ever going to break out of this mess? I don't want to be known as the "other woman" forever.'

'No Sanya, nothing of that sort is going to happen. This is just a small dent. Don't worry,' Lara advises.

Sanya fiddles with her phone to check her messages and BBMs.

'He hasn't even called or messaged,' she says quietly.

'Probably because that tiny bitch stole his phone,' I snort.

'Sanya, whether or not he calls or messages, you need to walk away now. Indian men never leave their wives, you know that,' Lara lectures gently.

'And dude, did you see her? I'd be scared to leave her,' I remark.

Sanya lets out a big sigh of defeat.

'Did you notice how calm and collected she was? I mean if it was me, I would have created a ruckus. She was so calm, like she had done this a few times. Maybe it's not the first time he's cheated,' Lara ponders aloud.

Sanya shrugs. 'I guess there are no fairytales in real life,' she comments softly.

We look at each other and fall silent in a subdued mood, thinking of Palak. And I think of my not-so-charming Prince. Men really are frogs.

'How did this start?' I ask, trying to hint towards: *did you not know he was fucking married?*

She closes her eyes, lets out a deep breath and begins, 'We met at an event and he was there alone. I had no idea who he was, but he brought me a drink and flirted with me throughout. He seemed mesmerized by me and seemed so genuine. I was completely blown away.'

It's easy to see why anybody would be mesmerized by Sanya—her beauty is unrivalled and she possesses a powerful charisma. It is not that hard to fall in love with her, but rather difficult to keep her satiated, keep up with her partying and her ambitions. She is a dynamic woman, and to be compatible with her one has to be an equally dynamic man, one who can sustain her appetite for life, and make the relationship for keeps. So far no one has met the mark.

'Sanjay is everything I want in a man; he is confident, alluring, smart and *funny!*' she stresses on 'funny' and smiles.

'No one has ever made me laugh this much, he is perfect. Well he *was* perfect,' she says bitterly.

'Except that he is married,' Lara comments gently. 'The tiny bitch beat you to him.'

Sanya nods in pain. 'And he kept pursuing me. I reminded him often that he is married, so we should not do this, but he kept insisting that he just needed a friend, someone to talk to, someone who understands him. He used the stereotypical married man dialogues, and I fell for it, because I was just too bloody attracted to him. We met for coffee and drinks first, and then we became conscious of people seeing us together, so one day, he got a room at a hotel as a "surprise" for me, and of course, he insisted that nothing will happen, but like, yeah right! I mean what do you expect me to do when there is a hell of an attractive guy who I'm falling in love with, some wine and a bed?' She smiles resentfully. 'It just never stopped since then. It's been almost a month now. We never talked about the future, or the reality, it was just a few hours of me, him and being us. Away from everything, like an escape. But I couldn't get out of it. I knew it would have to end one day, but I just kept holding onto a tiny hope that he would leave and come to me forever.' She falls silent for a second and then adds, 'But I guess that's not happening. It was just short-lived bliss.' She lays her head back and shuts her eyes while a few tears stream down.

I reach out for another piece of chocolate.

'It's fine, nothing a little piece of candy can't fix.'

She smiles and lays back further into her bed, 'I think I will finally sleep peacefully tonight.' She shuts her eyes. I pat her head and set the pillows comfortably around her.

Lara and I quietly move out from the bed, putting her phone on silent and allowing her to drift off to sleep.

EVERY WOMAN SHOULD KNOW WHEN TO TRY HARDER AND WHEN TO WALK AWAY

The day has finally arrived to get rid of Rajesh. It is now or never. I can't take it any more and I have run out of reasons to be with him. There is no blushing, no fluttering of the heart and definitely no happy smile. The happy smile only appears after many glasses of cheap wine! Sometimes things aren't always what they seem. And even though Rajesh and I are perfect on paper the reality cannot be further off.

Yes, it is time to do the deed.

I fiddle with my phone, trying to figure out how to break it to Rajesh. I take a deep breath as I dial his number.

He answers, 'Hi, I've been wondering where you disappeared!'

Get straight to the point Neha.

'So, I have been doing some thinking and I don't know if this is really working out well.'

Silence.

God, I am such a bitch. How can I be so ruthless?

'Rajesh, are you there? Will you say something?' I lose my confidence.

'Umm, yes I am listening. What is it that you want me to say?'

'I am not sure if you are really right for me.'

There I said it.

'What?' his voice rises.

Uh oh.

'Rajesh, I don't think I want to continue this relationship. I think we are in different places. Also, I really don't think we are right for each other.'

'Is this because I don't like your friends?' he sounds angry.

'No, it has nothing to do with that. There are many other factors involved.'

'Really? Look, you can meet your friends for a ladies' lunch or something like that. I did not say you cannot see them at all. I am just saying that I do not want to hang out with them all the time. And you have my friends to hang out with too. I am sure you will like them.'

He has friends?

'Rajesh, it has nothing to do with friends or anything. It's me. I don't think marriage is right for us, because neither of us will be happy in the long run. Your personality is really different, and you aren't as outgoing and all that, and I know it will always be a reason for us to fight. And most importantly, I feel you cannot seem to accept me the way I am.'

'Well, I am what I am,' he replies adamantly.

Losers use this line for hiding what they can't be.

I take another deep breath, 'I am sorry Rajesh.'

Silence.

'Rajesh?'

'Yeah, yeah, I'm here. Okay I get it, that's okay. Umm . . . well . . . I guess . . . that's it then.'

'Yeah . . .' I trail off, not knowing what else to say.

'Umm . . . I really did enjoy being with you Neha. I hope we can continue to be friends.'

'Yep,' I say, not offering anything more. There really is nothing else that I can add.

'Okay, so I guess I shall see you around?'

'Yeah, you take care. Thanks for understanding.'

Come on, end the conversation now.

'Sure, no worries, take care of yourself.' He pauses for a bit before he adds, 'You know, Neha, maybe you don't know what you are looking for yet. You need to grow up a little.'

'Excuse me?' I ask horrified.

'You have no right to dump me like this. It just proves that you are so immature and childish and you have to grow up yet. You are never gonna get a guy as good as me,' he is screaming now.

'Rajesh, I am sorry but I don't think you need to go that far.' I am so angry now I know I am bound to say things I will regret later.

'It's true and you know it. You are just being really stupid about this and are influenced by your slutty and dumb friends.'

'Rajesh, there is no reason whatsoever to insult my friends,' I reply sternly.

How dare he!

'You think I don't know about Sanya's affair? If your friends are like this, I'm sure you're the same. In fact, *I* am dumping *you*. I shouldn't have dated you for so long anyways!' he screeches.

That's it.

'Rajesh, that is enough!' I yell. 'You are an ungrateful, unpleasant jerk and you look like a frog. What you really are looking for is a mother and what I am looking for is a real man. And you are under no circumstance a real man. Goodbye.'

I shake with so much fury I almost jam the end call key of my BlackBerry.

Oh my God! Oh my God! Oh my God! Did I just say that? The bastard deserved it though. How dare he insult me and my friends? Who does he really think he is? Calling me immature!

I calm down a bit.

But I still said some awful things. I shattered his heart! I am definitely going to hell. But who cares anyways, the party in hell will probably be way more fun!

I smile sadly.

It's an end to something that could have been much greater.

I call Lara, 'I broke up with him!'

'Oh baby, I am sorry!'

'No, don't be, I'm fine. I feel much better now. I don't feel so burdened any more.' I pause, 'But, I am alone again.'

'Neha, don't worry. Have you told your parents yet?'

'No, not yet. But I will now. They're both home.'

'How did he take it?'

'Um, not so well. It got really heated and it ended with me telling him that he ain't a man!'

'NEHA! Are you serious?' Lara bursts out laughing. 'Okay sorry, don't worry about it. Do you need anything? Shall I come over?'

'No, it's fine. I will just check in with Sanya later tonight.'

'Okay, fine. Good luck with your mother!'

♆

When I enter the living room where Dad usually reads in the evening, I start to feel queasy again.

'Umm, Dad, I broke up with Rajesh.'

He slowly removes his reading glasses and looks up at me with concern, 'Are you okay?'

I take a deep breath and smile, 'Yes, I am, actually I have never felt more relieved!'

He smiles back, 'Then I am happy for you.' He pats his hand on the sofa seat next to him, motioning me to sit down.

'Do you feel like having ice cream?' I ask.

'Of course I do,' he stands up immediately, laying his book down with a feather bookmark on the page. 'Tell your mother,' he smiles with glee. Ice cream always gets him moving, even from his favourite book.

As if on cue, my mother enters. 'Tell me what?' she demands.

'We are going out for ice cream. Get ready.'

'What? No, Neha, you have been eating so much junk recently!' she shouts.

'She dumped Rajesh,' Dad smiles.

How did he figure out I dumped him?

I look at him and he winks back.

'What?' My mother's eyes widen in shock. 'Why? When? Oh come on, I think I need an ice cream now too,' she grumbles.

'I don't like him,' I state to no one in particular.

'Oh, so you are not upset about this?' asks my shocked mother.

'Nope!' I smile back.

'Then why do you need ice cream?'

'To celebrate!' I gush excitedly. 'Can we go to Sea Lounge? I want a banana split.'

'Mmm . . . and I would like a Knight Rider!' comments Dad as we exit our home.

🍸

My humungous banana split arrives along with Dad's Knight Rider while my mother settles with some herbal tea. We are a funny family. My mother always sits straight in the finest of clothes and jewellery and my father, bent over, is interested more in what's on his plate than around. And me, a lost child, trying to just do my thing without getting noticed. But that rarely happens with my mother around. While Dad and I love to be alone and enjoy our moments, my mother is always worrying and fussing.

'Tell me, Neha, what was wrong with this boy?' she asks pensively.

'He was just too much to handle. He had an issue with everything I did. And I don't know, it just didn't feel right. Plus, Mum, he asked the price of a *glass* of wine for me!'

I knew that would kill it for her!

My mother's eyes become even wider, 'He what?'

Bingo!

Dad smiles at me fondly, 'You see, love, maybe you should stay with me for the rest of your life!'

'Absolutely not!' screeches my mother. 'That is the worst idea ever!' her forehead tries to show worry, but the Botoxed skin refuses to crease. 'Wait, did you break it off? Or did he?' she asks.

'I did!' I reply indignantly. 'I even told him that I am looking for a man and he doesn't really qualify under that category!'

'Neha!' her eyes almost pop out like Rajesh's. She covers her face with her hands, 'How are you my daughter!'

'That's my girl!' My dad cracks up. 'Eat up!' He smiles widely, clearly proud of me.

As I devour my ice cream hurriedly, aware of Dad's eyes preying on my sundae, my mother fusses, 'Neha, there is ice cream all around your mouth. Eat properly.'

'What? Where?'

'Here,' she takes a napkin and wipes my mouth. 'Honestly, who celebrates a break-up? It's all these stupid Bollywood movies that are giving you such crazy ideas!'

'Hi Neha!' A man's voice calls out.

I look up to find Ishaan smiling amusedly at me.

Crap!

'Hi,' I say lamely, trying to grab the napkin from my mother's hand.

'Ishaan! How lovely to see you! How are you?' coos my ecstatic mother.

'I am good Sheila Aunty. Uncle, how are you? I see that you still have to take care of your little daughter!'

'I know, she just hasn't grown up!' says my mother while wiping my cheek.

'Our daughter is always going to be our little baby to us,' comments Dad, beaming at me.

Thank God for him!

'Oh yes of course, Neha is our little girl too! We always have to look out for her!' Ishaan chuckles.

The bastard!

I stare daggers at him. He grins even more.

'Good Lord, Neha! When will you grow up? Ishaan, why don't you join us?'

'Oh I'd love to, but I already ate the entire menu and have to leave now.'

'Another model waiting for you?' I ask sarcastically.

'No, I need to go home! I have an early start tomorrow. I don't think I need to tell you to enjoy your ice cream!' he laughs, pointing his finger to my chin.

'Oh, Neha,' my mother takes another napkin and starts rubbing my chin.

'Mum, stop it, I'll do it!'

'Okay, I have to go, but I'll see you around Neha. And it was nice to see you two after so long!'

'Bye Ishaan,' my mother coos.

'Bye,' my father and I say in unison.

Ishaan waves and walks off.

'Such a lovely boy! Why can't you be nicer to him, Neha? He is so nice, and it looks like he is fond of you!'

'Mum, he is a friend and that's it. And he only likes models. He doesn't go for the normal girls!'

'Oh well, I don't blame him. He is so handsome!'

'Dad! Make her stop!' I pout.

'Sheila, enough now, let the girl eat her ice cream. Neha, do you want some *chaat*?'

'Yes!' I reply, full of energy.

'Okay, one chaat coming right up for my girl!'

I grin at my mother who is clearly not so happy about the extra calories coming to the table.

🍸

After my lavish ice cream and late night snack I head straight to Sanya's apartment with a bottle of wine. I am shocked to see the state she is in when she opens the door. She has sunken eyes and her dark circles become prominent against her fair skin. She smiles weakly and gives me a tight hug.

Sanya's break ups have never been this bad.

'I dumped Rajesh!' I smile, hoping to cheer her up. I show her the bottle.

She takes it and bursts out laughing, 'Let's celebrate!'

From the kitchen she brings out two glasses and packets of crisps. As we settle down in her room, I dig into my favourite place, her candy drawer, while Sanya pours out the wine.

'Cheers! To mend broken hearts and to heal them for new beginnings!' she giggles.

After a few good sips, Sanya asks, 'So, what did he say? Was he shocked?'

'Yeah, I think so. He kept thinking it was because of you guys. He kinda lectured me about how he is what he is and he isn't going to change and that I should meet my friends just during a ladies' lunch!' Sanya continues laughing. 'You found Rajesh rather amusing, didn't you?' I raise my eyebrows, smiling.

'Oh yes!' she says through peals of laughter! 'He was just so funny! The ideal Friday night *bakra*! He's definitely someone I'd have for breakfast!' She passes me some peanut M&Ms.

'Oh, I don't doubt that at all!' I imagine Sanya grilling him and then tearing him apart with a steak knife. 'You know what else I said to him?' I smile, looking forward to lifting up her mood. 'I told him that I am looking for a man and he isn't one, and that he is actually looking for a mother.'

Sanya clutches her stomach and rolls over laughing.

'I also told him that he looks like a frog!' I join in her laughter, still trying to digest the fact that I had actually insulted him so badly. 'And that he is an ungrateful and unpleasant jerk!' I sip more wine. 'And I wasn't even drunk! I said all this to him being completely sober!' I smile proudly.

Sanya wipes her tears away and finally says, 'I am going to send Rajesh a bouquet of flowers. I mean seriously, how else could we be so entertained at this moment?' she giggles, gurgling down her glass.

'I agree,' I smile sadly. 'You know, I really thought that he had potential. I didn't fall in love with him, but I still did not want to break it off either. And I think he did really like me. I feel guilty.'

'No, Neha, you shouldn't feel bad,' says Sanya firmly. 'I think you were just going with the flow. When you came with him at Aer, you didn't look happy. I felt like you were really making an effort to be happy and feel comfortable. Have you seen Lara glow whenever she is with Ashish? Even after so many years? And all that shit with his family? I mean come on, I would have left the guy by now, but she hasn't. And that's love.' She adds quietly, 'It took a bashing from the wife for me to leave Sanjay. Otherwise I don't think I could have let go.'

I pat her shoulder, 'Hmm, I guess so. But he did like me and I was rude to him, so I can't help feeling bad. God, why is it so hard? Nothing ever works out for me. I think I'm gonna be single for the rest of my life.'

'That makes two of us. At least we have each other!' Sanya grins. 'But seriously, Neha, it will come when you least expect it. It just happens. And when it does you won't even know what hit you,' she says wisely.

'You wanna go for a walk? I've been cooped up in my room for almost a week! I need some air.'

'Of course, let's go. Take the M&Ms,' I agree, finishing off my drink.

We venture out into the familiar polluted air of Mumbai. Sanya and I walk downhill on Alta Mount road towards Kemps Corner. The damp November night envelopes us in a comforting silence as we munch on candy, walking past large residential buildings.

'Oh my God!' Sanya gasps in terror and pulls me back into the side of a building entrance and we crouch uncomfortably behind the gate.

'What are you doing?' I exclaim.

'Quiet!' Sanya hisses. 'That's Sanjay's car,' she whispers, holding my hand tightly.

We peer out from the shadows to watch Sanjay climbing out of the driver's seat of his black BMW. A tall and voluptuous woman stands by the kerbside with her hands on her hips, her back towards us. She looks familiar, but she is definitely not tiny Asha. Sanjay walks around to the lady and tries appeasing her with all sorts of hand gestures. He finally pulls her into a tight embrace, caressing her back and head while she succumbs into his broad arms. They pull away after what feels like a millennium and the woman starts to walk into the building, giving us a good side view of her curvaceous body in a figure, hugging dress. He runs after her and pulls her back into a passionate kiss.

Sanya's fingernails dig into my palms as we both gasp at the glimpse of the woman.

The strangely familiar woman is none other than Monica the bitch, wife to Harry darling!

She waves goodbye as Sanjay drives away, presumably back to his wife or another mistress. She stands glowing in the dark with a rare 60-watt smile.

What is it about this guy?

'Come on,' Sanya grabs my hand and we venture back into the streetlight towards Monica.

'No, no,' I whisper in fear.

'Yes, she should know we know!' she replies determinedly.

Despite my grappling fear, a sense of excitement encompasses me.

This may just become my blackmail card at work.

Sanya clears her throat loudly as we approach a startled Monica. She turns around with her eyes wide in fear and freezes at the sight of us. Sanya stops abruptly, with me following her actions, and offers her a sweet smile. Monica scans us up and down while slowly regaining her composure and proceeds to walk into her apartment block, pretending not to have noticed. I wait for her to be out of sight before I can react in any way. I glance at Sanya uncertainly but she bursts out laughing.

'She looked like a deer caught in the headlights!' Sanya laughs. I silently sigh with relief.

'Shit! Monica and Sanjay? Did you have any idea? Does a thing like fidelity even exist any more?'

Sanya quiets down, 'No, it doesn't. Man, was I stupid! What the fuck was I thinking?' A tear trickles down her flawless cheek.

I clasp my arm around her shoulders as we turn back towards home, offering her another M&M.

'No need to regret something that once made you smile. At least you know what love is now.'

'Hmm,' she sniffles. We walk back home. Our initial comforting silence turns into a stunned and overwhelmed one.

Sanya starts laughing again, 'Monica? Really? I mean, I know he likes big boobs but come on, those plastic jugs are humongous, dude! That's just gross! I'm glad I'm out of this now. God knows how many more there are.'

'I don't know, but trying to handle three women at a time, especially ones like you three, requires some skill!' We laugh at the absurdity of the thought.

'You know, I don't think I'm quite cut out for relationships. I can't do what Lara is doing. That's just too much shit for me to deal with. I just want something simple, where we like each other, get married and everyone is happy,' I comment.

'Neha, nothing even remotely related to love, romance or marriage is simple. It all gets complicated. The deeper you get involved, the more complicated it is going to be. And that's the beauty of it. It's a test to see if you really are meant to be or not,' Sanya lectures.

I stare at Sanya scornfully, 'Sanya? Is that really you? Are you preaching about love?'

Sanya laughs, 'Yes I am. I know it sounds weird to hear something so profound from me, but I do know a thing or two.'

I shake my head, smiling as we enter our building gate.

Things really do change when men enter women's lives.

IF ONLY YOUTH KNEW; IF ONLY AGE COULD

It's Saturday night. And Palak is ready to roll. You can see it in her eyes that she is yearning to fade away into her own world. Palak's miseries have been getting worse each day; she is feeling torn between two very important priorities. Apparently, Raj is in a miserable mess as well, quite believable and typical; the male species only realize what they're missing after it's gone. I would have any day picked a faithful boyfriend over a hardworking job which makes you slog on weekends too, but then again, I never really understood Palak's dedication to her job in the first place. Sanya is even worse; she doesn't even understand the fundamental concept of reaching work at 9 a.m., dedication is an alien notion altogether.

Lara's boutique is a precious little haven in the centre of Kemps Corner in south Mumbai. Her studio is a piece of royalty. Hues of rich maroons, deep blues and purples adorn velvet sofas, curtains and trinkets. Majestic gold-embossed wallpaper covers the walls while crystal chandeliers hang low from the ceiling. Wide mirrors in heavy antique gold frames are strategically placed for customers to admire themselves in Lara's creations. Gold racks hold magnificent pieces of clothing, evening gowns, cocktail dresses and saris studded with semi-precious stones and other glittering stuff. An ornate coffee table lies at the centre of the sofa set with a bunch of fashion magazines strewn about. Anyone entering Lara's boutique is treated like royalty and doesn't leave without bags full of regal outfits that are certain to make heads turn. And I don't say this just because she is my friend!

The back room is a different story altogether with tables loaded with material, fabric and lace. There is another comfy seating area with large sofas relegated only for us, and a locked cabinet which when opened, reveals an extensive bar with bottles of vodka and our favourite wines.

Lara is working late and so we decided to bring pizza and have a night in, especially since everyone is in such a subdued mood.

Lara enters the back room with a mischievous smile, 'Guys, I think I have something that you all really need right now!' She takes out a cigarette pack and opens it to show the contents. Inside are two neatly rolled fat joints.

'Just what I need!' I exclaim with glee.

'I got it from Rajiv!' she laughs, her eyes sparkling with anticipation. 'I got two for us to share. Come on, we'll all feel better! And, I have got chocolate cake!'

'Chocolate cake?' My eyes light up.

Palak gets up and says, 'Come on, let's light it.'

'Okay, but do you want to see Ashish's mother's outfit first? I think it would better if we see it before we get high!' Lara giggles.

She opens a cupboard and out comes a hideous brown lehenga with gaudy embroidery and green and gold sequins.

'That is disgusting! Who on earth would wear that?' I exclaim. 'I'm no fashionista but even I know that it would be a crime to wear that!'

'Yeah, I know. I mean, I know they hate me, but seriously why go to this extent to insult me? I told Divya that this colour won't look good. So she went and told her mother some other kind of story which got her pissed again. So she went and got it done from one of her so-called designer friends, you know, the unqualified kind who made one garment and got fake complimented and so opened a shop the very next day! Then Riya came by a few days back and dropped this off and basically ordered me to make the blouses because the mother didn't like the original one!' Lara rants on. 'Seriously, just bloody talk to me directly and all this can be avoided!' she exclaims in frustration.

'Wow, I really need the spliff now. Put it away or I might end up blazing it,' says Palak. She smiles her first smile of the week as she takes a long drag.

Thirty minutes later and two joints burnt to ashes, the four of us are profoundly happy, giggling and munching on cheese pizza as Sanya searches for a vodka bottle in Lara's big stash. A complete contrast to how the night had started off.

A baked Sanya gives a brilliant idea, 'Let's go clubbing!'

'What? Now?' I question.

'Yes, now, it's a Saturday night. Let's go all out, like a bunch of teenagers. I know, let's go to Prive. We can dance on the table tops!' her eyes gleam with mischief.

'Okay, I'm in,' says Palak, stuffing a slice of pizza into her mouth. Two seconds later she picks up her vodka and gulps it down in one go.

Being stoned definitely has its effects. 'Me too,' I hear myself saying, 'But, I'm not dressed for clubbing.'

'Ooh, I can take care of that!' exclaims Lara, delighted at the thought of dressing us up.

'Give me your skankiest outfit. We are going to be competing with the slutty sixteen-year-olds tonight,' blurts out a laughing Palak.

The nightclub we intend to grace tonight is generally filled with extremely skinny high school teenagers, giving all of us a mighty complex: one of the reasons why we like to avoid nightclubs and stick to more sober and 'classier' bars.

Lara heads into her storage cupboard and comes out with heaps of clothes in various colours. 'Here Palak, this is for you,' she smiles excitedly. She pulls out a tiny sea-green satin dress. Palak rushes to change into it, clearly thrilled at having a skanky little thing to wear. She comes out wearing very little. The sleeveless dress barely covers her bottom and a deep scooped backline shows off her slender behind. But she keeps her ponytail and glasses on.

'Whoa!' gushes Lara, proud at the transformation her little creation does to Palak. A stoned Palak starts giggling and states, 'I am going to have loads of fun tonight and not even think about Hong Kong. Now where's my drink? And for the record, I think we should blaze more often!'

Raising my eyebrows towards Lara, I ask what's in store for me. She pulls out a hot pink fitted strapless dress with black trimmings, slightly too short for my liking. But what the hell, everyone's getting skanky, so why not me!

For Sanya these are normal clothes. She needs something different. She rummages through Lara's wardrobe and comes out with a tiny cream-coloured silk dress, printed with large red flowers. She strips unconsciously in front of us and slips on the dress. She looks smoking hot! The barely-there straps further accentuate her toned shoulders and the dress fits her like a glove.

Lara gets into a blue sequined top teamed with black booty hot pants. While I devour the chocolate cake with Palak, Sanya finishes up the last slice. Lara pours out the remaining vodka into our glasses. *Clink.* Within ten minutes there isn't a drop of vodka or crumb of the cake left.

We stumble into the car and then stumble back out outside Prive with great difficulty. Palak tries to pull down her green dress to cover her bottom but in vain. She gives up halfway and starts strutting her stuff like it's her job! Around us are fifteen-year-olds dressed in even less (if that were even possible) staring at us. We really look out of place but when one is high everything seems funny and the four of us can't stop laughing

Upon entering the club we are welcomed with a crowd of teeny boppers and high school kids and we head straight to the bar. Sanya climbs over to get the attention of the bartender. He comes rushing to us, undoubtedly because Sanya's flailing boobs almost fall out of her tight dress.

Sanya shouts over the music, 'Four tequila shots.'

When they come she turns around to hand us our shots and as we raise our glasses to clink them, Sanya toasts, 'To wives and mistresses—may they never meet.'

We burst out laughing before gulping down the alcohol. But it isn't enough. I ask the bartender for eight more shots, sensing that it would be hard to get more later with the number of teeny boppers beating us to the bar.

Now each of us has two shots in our hands.

I shout over the music, 'For getting high and plastered tonight and reliving our sweet sixteen parties with cupcakes and pink frills. Damn, times have changed!' Gulp. Another one down.

Lara lifts the second shot, 'For dancing *on* tables tonight.' Third one down.

Palak insists she should get a chance to toast as well and so starts to wave at the bartender for one more round while flashing her bottom as she reaches over the bar. Had we been sober, we would have definitely made the effort to cover her. *Had* we been sober!

'Screw the fucking bastards that broke our hearts!' and she tosses the vodka into her mouth before we even get to clink our glasses.

Just when we put our shot glasses down and it seems impossible that we can drink any more, the DJ announces, 'Girls who dance on the bar, get free drinks,' and a lot of drunk girls start shrieking. Including us.

As Palak takes the chance to climb onto the barstool to get pulled up to the bar, I am still looking on in shock.

Oh what the hell, why not join in the revelry? In my drunken and delirious state I get pulled up by someone on to the bar top.

Somewhere around the song *Whine Up*, I step on something slippery, which sends me flying off the bar and I find myself flat on the floor, trying to regain my balance clutching onto a barstool for my life.

A strong grip holds me by the shoulders and steadies me before pulling me up.

'You okay?' A voice from behind asks.

I turn around, wide eyed, to see my saviour, still reeling from the shock and feeling disillusioned and frazzled. I see a tall, handsome man, with a slight stubble, a cleft on the jaw line, and short curly hair. I smile lazily, not making an effort to get up, trying to figure out how I can hug and kiss my saviour until I recognize the face: Ishaan.

He looks me up and down amusedly and smirks, 'You should be careful, you're not sixteen!'

'Oh my God, I am going to fall again!' I go paranoid as I hold on to him tighter. 'Wait, what did you say?' I stop in alarm.

He did not just say that.

He steadies me again and smiles at me, 'Celebrating again, are we?'

My hand itches to slap him, but instead I hear myself shout back, 'Shut up. Where are your models?'

He looks up at Lara, Sanya, Palak and then me and replies, 'Looks like I don't need any models today, you girls look better than them!'

'Ohh, I get it, you're here to pick up sixteen-year-olds, you sick bastard,' I giggle.

'Well, I could say the same thing about you lot, here to pick up sixteen-year-old boys,' he says pointing at the bar top. I look up to see where he is pointing and find Palak still grinding with Lara and Sanya making out with a younger looking guy.

I gasp, lifting my hand to my mouth in worry.

He laughs, 'Don't worry, she's just having some fun.'

I look over in disgust, horrified that he would allow a friend to continue such debauchery. But he looks serious and assuring, which can only mean that he knew about her affair.

Well, I guess a little fun won't hurt her.

'So, what exactly are you doing here?' I mellow down. 'This isn't your usual kind of pick-up joint. And are you alone?' I feign shock.

'Well, my younger cousin is visiting from Delhi and she is meeting up with her friends here. And I wanted to keep an eye on her. They're bloody fifteen! I can't believe they're allowed to go clubbing at this age. I don't ever remember being fifteen and taking whisky shots! Though, they do seem to fit into this environment much better than we do,' he nods at the crowd.

I look at him in surprise, 'Oh, and how old are you, Uncle?'

He looks down at me, 'I'm twenty-eight.' And then he frowns, 'How old are you?'

'Excuse me! You're not supposed to ask a girl her age.'

He laughs, 'Oh, so now you're a girl?'

I reach out to punch him, annoyed and not interested in carrying on this conversation any more. He ducks and I start to walk away, aggravated, but he pulls me back instantly, 'Hey, hey, I was just kidding around, of course you look like a girl. Who else wears pink? Besides, I have no one else to hang out with.'

'Ohh . . . so you just want to hang out with me for time pass.'

'Of course not! I do enjoy your company. Plus I haven't had a chance to talk to you in a while. Especially since *Rajesh* was around!' he mockingly stresses on Rajesh's name.

'What is that supposed to mean?'

'Oh nothing. I'm just saying, you have been quiet recently and you are always glaring at me these days. Actually, you amuse me!'

I look at him in shock, my temper rising, 'Amuse you? Am I to stay here to be insulted?'

He laughs again, 'No, I mean it in a nice way. You're witty and funny, and you are a lot of fun to be with. I mean, who else goes out and celebrates a break up with their parents?' he smiles at me. He takes me by the arm and calls the bartender for two glasses of champagne. 'Here you go; a more sophisticated adult drink.'

I purse my lips, still not entirely okay at being called a 'man' first and then 'amusing', but proceed to sip the champagne all the same. Hey, you can't say no to booze, can you?

'Wait, you must toast.'

'What?'

'You must always clink your champagne flute or else you won't have sex for a year,' he explains gravely.

'Oh, of course, and wouldn't that be such a big catastrophe, what with all those models that need your servicing!' I smile sarcastically.

'Servicing?' His eyes crinkle up as he belts out a hearty laugh, 'God, you have some vocabulary!'

I frown at him, not understanding what he finds so funny.

He continues, 'And you make it sound like a bad thing. Wouldn't you like to get "serviced" too? I mean not necessarily by me but by someone.'

'Necessarily?' I redden, 'Never ever by you!'

He laughs, 'Okay, so you would like to be serviced by someone at least.'

'Shut up, here, cheers,' I clink with his glass and gulp down a large sip of bubbly.

'Stop being so grumpy now, you were being so giggly ten minutes ago, what happened? Did your high evaporate?' he teases.

Ugh, how does he figure everything out?

'Come on, Neha, relax, you're always so uptight—do you know how good you look when you relax? Or do you really hate me so much?'

'Oh, I don't hate you!' I lighten up. 'I just, I just . . . Well, I don't know, I don't like shallow guys.'

'And what makes you think I am shallow?' asks Ishaan calmly.

'Because you are always with models, or model-like women, and each time I see you, there is a different one. And I have never seen you actually have a conversation with any one of them, they usually just stand next to you and sip on one glass of champagne the entire night, while you chat and joke with the rest of us. I mean clearly, you are only attracted to beautiful things, and that's where it ends!'

He laughs again; he really seems to find me amusing!

'No, that is not true, I don't sleep with all of them, and I do admire intelligence, wit and humour. I just like to go with the flow! And as of now I would like to fish in shallow waters; easy entry and easy exit. When I am ready I shall go for the bigger fish in the deep water where there is difficult entry and no exit! And just a FYI, I don't run after them, good-looking women come on to me as well!' he points out.

'Okay, whatever! It's none of my business!' and I take the last sip of the remaining champagne.

'Wow, you definitely don't drink like a model! One more?'

I laugh, 'Yes, I don't and I will take that as a compliment. But no thank you, I'll have one later,' I smile back.

He isn't too bad after all! Quite tolerable. Or maybe I am still high.

'So, how is your work going? Do you still put in a hundred hours a week?' Ishaan works as an investment banker at a multinational. 'You know, you are probably one of the few people I know who work hard and play harder. It's quite commendable,' I smile.

Okay, I'm complimenting Ishaan, I am definitely high!

'Oh yes, it's pretty intense, but I like it. In fact I love it at the bank. The client I am working with currently is pretty interesting, so it's good. What about you? How's Rita treating you?' Rita is clearly famous.

'Pretty all right. It's the clients that we work with that are impossible, especially Harry and Monica! It is fun sometimes, and other times it's frustrating.' Then I remember, 'Oh, I got an offer to be promoted if I work hard!' I giggle.

Hmm . . . Strange, I hadn't mentioned this to Rajesh.

'Oh! Finally, I am impressed!' I pout at his response and he laughs, 'It's okay, you are our baby, you don't need to work!'

'Are you calling me a loser?' I ask seriously.

He laughs harder and bends over to hug me and kiss my cheek, 'Of course not, my child, you are our delicate darling!'

I touch my nose, wondering if that is what he is referring to.

'Stop it! I am not talking about your beautiful nose!' he says sternly. 'So what exactly happened to that wimp you brought with you to Aer?'

'He wasn't so bad,' I defend Rajesh. 'I mean, come on, how can you guys all judge so much?'

'Well, to be honest, you deserve better,' he says sincerely. I raise an eyebrow. 'Well, I wouldn't say someone as good as me, but at least a few levels below me,' he teases.

I roll my eyes, 'Okay, I give up!'

He grins cheekily then asks, 'Are you desperate to get married?'

'Oh God! No! I would first like to meet someone who isn't half as bad, you know what I mean?'

Ishaan nods understandingly.

Dude, doesn't his stubble look good? NEHA! What is wrong with you? Stop ogling at Ishaan, of all people! He only likes the skinny and 6-feet tall bimbos—and you are neither skinny nor tall and you most certainly are not a bimbo.

I pout again, 'Actually, I really just want a boyfriend who takes me out to dinner and we party together and then he can drop me back home!'

'Ah! Well, you will find hundred such people who will be willing to do that for you!'

I look scornfully at him.

'Don't worry, you're still young,' he says. I raise my eyebrow, to which he responds, 'Well, you're not sixteen, but you aren't thirty either, so relax.'

The casual conversation begins to take a weird turn, making me shift uncomfortably, usually a signal to change the topic.

Think, Neha, think! Shit, why am I so high?

Meanwhile a young teenage girl comes up to Ishaan and pats his shoulder, 'Okay, I'm done, I want to go home now.' Her eyes are droopy and she looks fairly wasted.

She realizes that I am standing next to Ishaan and turns around to eye me closely before giving Ishaan a confused look, 'But she is not a model!'

I burst out laughing. My point that Ishaan is shallow has just been proven!

'You clearly have a reputation!' I chuckle.

'Hey, Priya, she happens to be a good friend of mine. And I think someone has had a bit too much to drink,' warns Ishaan, slightly embarrassed. I think I sense some annoyance in his voice or I could be too drunk and stoned.

Tipsy Priya starts to lean on Ishaan and begins to whine, 'Can we go now?'

'Why? Are all your friends starting to leave too?'

'Yeah, kinda, they're actually all too wasted,' she tries to state matter-of-factly but ends up in a long slur.

'Oh God,' he sighs exasperatedly. 'Okay, let's go. Will you be okay, Neha?'

I smile, 'Yes thank you, bye!' Ishaan rolls his eyes and gives an apologetic look.

'I'll see you around,' he says as he hugs me and kisses my cheek again.

As he leaves, Lara, Palak and Sanya get off the bar, soaked in sweat and smiling dreamily.

'We are tired,' proclaims Lara. 'Was that Ishaan?'

'I want to go home,' says Sanya drowsily.

'I am going to Hong Kong,' slurs Palak. 'Fuck, I am going to Hong Kong!' Palak's voice strengthens. 'I am going to have to start all over again after four bloody years. Four bloody years!'

'Okay, let's go home now before we all start getting paranoid,' says Lara.

I glance at my watch. It is only 1.30 a.m..

Damn, we're really getting old!

On the drive back home Palak repeats, 'It's over. It's fucking over,' and bursts out laughing as tears of sadness roll down her face. Then she shakes her head, 'Everything is going to be all right.'

Sanya rests her head on Palak's shoulders, 'We are all going to be okay.'

EVERYONE CRIES; SOME JUST HIDE THEIR TEARS

The early mornings and evenings after a break up are always the hardest. No more good morning messages, sleepy wake-up calls, or phone kisses to awaken me from my slumber. Or the end-of-a-rough-day therapeutic phone call and the comfort of being in his arms or holding his hand. A feeling of emptiness lingers on for what seems like forever. Despite our differences and our incompatibility, I had grown if not attached, quite used to Rajesh. Truth be told, I miss him. And suddenly I cannot stand romantic movies, I cannot bear seeing couples holding hands and anything remotely lovey dovey turns me off. I don't want to be reminded of my singlehood.

And to top it all when I enter the office, Nisha and Tanya approach me with stress written all over their faces. I can hear Rita yelling at the top of her voice from her cabin.

'What happened?'

'Harry happened! Look at this article,' Tanya shoves a newspaper on my face.

Indian Express, front page:

Real estate mogul under investigation for illegal land acquisitions

Harry Construction Ltd is reportedly under investigation by the central and state investigative agencies.

Harjeet Chaddha, also known as Harry, the managing director of the public company is also being investigated by the US authorities for alleged tax fraud and tax evasion worth US$20 million. Harry is an Indian national who started a small venture in the real estate segment in San Jose, California, in 1997 and later with growing success shifted base to Los Angeles, California. He led a high-profile life mingling with celebrities, the rich and famous. He and his wife, Monica, lived in a palatial mansion in the posh locality of Beverly Hills, rubbing shoulders with the likes of Arnold Schwarzenegger and Oprah Winfrey.

However in 2008 the business went bust during the US real estate crisis and Chaddha shifted base to India to continue in the same business—real estate, and ventured prominently into the Mumbai high life. However, Chaddha has frequent run ins with the authorities over building projects on illegal or disputed lands. The latest project by the company, which costs approximately Rs 150 crores, is being sealed off until further notice.

'I knew it! I just knew it! Our conspiracy theory was true!' I laugh.

'Neha! Stop laughing! We may lose this account! We're supposed to have prevented this.'

'Yeah right! Harry can't do without Rita!' I smirk. 'But damn, this is really bad publicity, isn't it?'

'You think?' Tanya asks me scornfully. 'Rita has been yelling at everyone since this morning. I don't think the reporter who wrote this is gonna last long. But this is just the beginning. The other papers are going to get it tomorrow. We are gonna need to send out a press note ASAP.'

'Where is Monica? Is she coming in?'

'Yep! And so is Harry. We need to hear their whole story before we do anything. I assume the legal department will be coming in too.'

Monica bustles into the office in another one of her inappropriate work attires: skin-tight black wraparound dress which swells up her cleavage and exposes her thighs, black sunglasses and black five-inch pumps. Harry follows in a sweat-drenched white outfit. The black and white duo walk straight into Rita's chambers without knocking. Rita ushers them back out into the conference room.

'Tanya!' she calls out. I diligently rush behind Tanya.

As Monica sits down, angrily throwing the newspaper on the table, she yells, 'How dare they not mention me enough! And why did they not mention any of the charity and philanthropic work I do? How preposterous! These bloody reporters just don't get their facts right!'

'Charity wo . . .?' I trail off confusedly.

Monica glares angrily, 'All those charity events I attend. Tanya, prepare a damn press release right now and I want you to highlight all the good stuff I do. *With* my photograph!'

I raise my eyebrows, recalling her promiscuity.

She must have also suddenly remembered the incident. She calmly repeats, 'Tanya, let me know when you get it done.'

'Monica, baby, this is not the time . . .' Harry begins.

'Oh shut up, Harry. The last time you said you would handle it you couldn't, which is why we had to pack up and come here. I will do all the thinking and strategic planning from now on,' she yells.

Maybe I can go get coffee for everyone? That would make me so much more useful.

Monica tones down her voice, 'Rita, prepare a statement for the press stating the questioning was just a routine activity by the government and that we are cooperating. There are no legal issues and we are perfectly stable. We do not want our share prices to drop. It already has come down by 7 per cent in the last hour.'

Damn, I'm impressed!

'Rita, get us a few interviews in the social magazines like *Society*, *Hello* or *Verve* to show off our charity works and basically what great people we are,' Monica continues. 'I have already spoken to our legal department and my lawyers have assured me that the seal will be lifted within twenty-four hours.'

Harry sinks deeper into his chair as he accepts his defeat.

'Now, I'd like to leave this mess to you to handle as that is what I pay you lot to do. I have a facial appointment to catch.' Monica picks up her black Hermès Birkin and storms out haughtily, forgetting she had brought her husband with her!

Rita walks over to a sullen Harry to comfort him.

'Harry darling, do not worry. This is hardly a bump. We will sort it out. And remember, this is India—anything can be managed with a little string-pulling here and there.'

'I hope so!' Harry buries his head into his hands. 'I can't go through this again, I am too old. The local gangsters are after me too! And I almost lost Monica the last time; I can't lose her now. She is my third wife!'

All of us shift uncomfortably in our seats, including the senior management. Rita motions us to leave, saving him from further embarrassment. We quietly slip out of the room to begin the mammoth amount of work that lies ahead of us.

Y

I barely manage to gulp down an uninteresting supper alone and crawl into bed when my phone rings.

It's Ishaan. I check the time, its 10 p.m..

Probably to gloat about a hot date he has tonight.

'Hello!' greets Ishaan pleasantly.

'Hi, what's up?' I wonder why he's calling. It feels weird talking to a man who isn't Rajesh at the end of the day.

'I am trying to figure out what you're doing on a Friday night at home?'

'Huh? How do you know I'm home?' My voice rises.

He laughs, 'I don't, I was just assuming. And I assumed right!'

'Asshole!' I grumble.

'Actually, I called to ask how Palak and Sanya are doing, and if there is anything I can do.'

'Oh,' I feel guilty for doubting him. 'Yeah, neither is doing too well. But there isn't much we can do. Have you seen Raj recently? We have no idea what's going on with him.'

'No. He has just gone MIA. But we know he is not fine.' He pauses before he says, 'He does love her, you know.'

'Yes, we know that, but we don't get why he doesn't want to commit to a future together. It makes no sense.'

'No idea! If I was dating someone for so long and was one hundred per cent committed, I would definitely ask her to marry me by now.'

'Ah, but that's the difference, you are incapable of being committed!'

'No, that's not true! I can commit if I want to,' he says defensively. 'Get off my case!' he grumbles.

'Sorry.'

'And are you okay?' he asks gently.

His question stuns me. 'Huh?' I take more than a few seconds to recover, 'Yeah, I'm fine.'

'Are you sure?' he sounds genuinely concerned.

'Yes. I am, thank you,' I smile.

'Think on the bright side, you no longer have to worry about your husband drinking cosmopolitans with your girlfriends!' he laughs.

I can't help but laugh good-naturedly, 'I knew this wasn't going to remain a secret for very long.'

'This should *not* remain a secret. We should definitely spread the word to warn his new candidates though I doubt many other girls take alcohol as seriously or in fact drink the way you lot do!' I giggle in agreement. It is true, very few girls at our age enjoy their liquor the way we do.

'How was your day?' he asks.

'It was bad!' I grumble. 'We are in the midst of a crisis management situation for our client and his wife is a super bitch! I really hate working!'

'What about the promotion?'

Wow! He remembers!

'Blah! I don't know. I really don't want all the extra responsibility!'

'Oh, Neha! When will you grow up?'

'I don't want to grow up!' I reply stubbornly.

Ishaan laughs, 'Don't worry, you don't have to, I'm here!'

I laugh even more at the thought of him being of any use to me.

Our conversation floats on various topics, from bitching about Rajesh and Sanjay, to the latest movies, food and restaurants.

'It's Friday night, how come you are not out?' I ask, suddenly realizing that we have been talking for over an hour.

'Is there a law which forces me to be out every night of the week?'

'Of course there is! Whatever will happen to all those models then? Or wait, you don't have a hot date tonight? Oh good Lord! I am flabbergasted!' I scream, feigning shock.

'Yeah, I do in fact; I have two models to choose from. I'm trying to decide! One of them was just on the cover of some magazine and the other just became the face of something, I forget. But both are hot. Whom shall I pick?'

'You are impossible! You really think of every girl as a piece of ass and think you can play around with as many girls as you can handle. Don't you? I hate your kind,' I vent out at Ishaan.

'Yes, that's right, Neha, I am a huge ass player; a different girl every night! And that is exactly why I am talking to you over the phone on a Friday night!'

His comment stops me.

That is correct. Why is he talking to me on a Friday night? Instead of being out at a party with one of those bimbos I always see him with. And why the hell am I talking to him for so long? Especially when he manages to pull every nerve in my body? But why is HE talking to me? It doesn't make sense.

'Okay fine, whatever, stop talking now.'

He laughs back, 'Okay, well you go to sleep now and take care of yourself. Call me if you need anything.'

'Yes, yes, fine,' I reply, upset now that the conversation has to end so soon.

'And for the record, I'm not a player. The day I meet *the* girl I'm gonna be committed forever.'

'Sure!'

'Goodnight, Neha.'

'You too, have fun on your date!'

'Oh, I am not going. I am going to try to sleep too.'

'What? Why?' I ask baffled.

'Well, while you talked non-stop for the past hour, the other two got tired of being on call wait for so long.'

'Ohhh . . . oops . . . sorry,' I apologize with an evil grin.

I am not sorry at all. I just saved the 'small fish'!

He laughs in good spirit, 'No, it's okay, you can make it up to me some time later. Goodnight, baby!'

Baby?

He hangs up before I can respond.

Baby? Hmm . . . No Neha, it's Ishaan. It is in his nature to flirt. He doesn't mean anything. Why am I thinking too much about it? The thing about Ishaan is that you never know what he really means.

Before I do anything stupid or think any further, I dial Palak's number.

Palak grunts into the phone.

'Hi, how are you?'

'Okay.'

'Do you feel better?'

'Not really.'

'Palak, have you really thought about it? Maybe you should give him a chance?'

'What for? To hear false promises? Does he not realize what he is putting me through? I kept quiet about marriage for so long thinking that I don't want to put pressure on him and felt confident that it will all work out. Now it's his turn and he doesn't want to do it. He thinks this whole thing is a joke. I'm just really glad that it happened now. If this Hong Kong thing hadn't sprung up I would have never known and would have been hanging onto a loose thread forever. It would have never occurred to me to ask such shit. It's a big revelation and I'm relieved that it happened now rather than later.'

'But you love him Palak. Can you just let him go like that? And you know that he loves you too.'

'So what if I love him. I need security now. And if my love has no security, there is no point in being with that person. And I'm only getting older. When will it ever be the right time for him to get married if not now?'

'And the fact that he loves you means nothing?'

'A relationship does not just begin and end with love. There are so many other factors. And right now, whether he even loves me is questionable. If he loves me, the least he can do is provide me with this kind of a commitment. It's not such a big step for us at this stage. We've been together for so many years, I can't even count any more. I really think I was just a convenient option for him to be with and he had just gotten used to me.'

'Okay, okay, you have a point. I agree. Calm down. Now tell me all about Hong Kong,' I try to steer the conversation away from Raj.

Palak delves aggressively into the topic and continues ranting for an hour. She really is keen on getting the hell out of here. But I don't blame her. She had spent the last four years with Raj in Mumbai; every nook and corner has a memory of him. It would be unbearable.

Actually we are all crying a little inside for Palak and Raj. They had been the perfect couple and theirs was the ideal relationship with honesty, trust, compatibility and love. This rift between them has shaken us and forced us all to question ourselves and our relationships. Well, not me any more. There are no guarantees in life. Nothing ever goes according to plan and rules are always meant to be broken. Sometimes playing it safe becomes one the riskiest choices we can ever make because no one really knows what is going to happen.

'You know, I just don't want to be hanging around for things to happen when they are not even in my hands. I think it's time to take control of my life and do what I must. There really isn't anything else I can do. I mean come on, even Lara and Ashish have gotten engaged despite his family harassing her and we all know what a crazy relationship they have. They fight so much, they are totally different people and their families are as alike as the North and South Poles. Yet they made it through. And me and Raj? We almost never fight, our families approve, and we are really compatible etcetera, etcetera. What more do we need? He's just afraid of the word "marriage" and I should have heard the warning bells before, but I blindly ignored them without thinking at all.'

She has a point. To any outsider, Lara and Ashish just do not make sense. They are as different as chalk and cheese, but their love is so strong we know they will make it through anything.

Of course, Palak is doing the right thing from her point of view. But what about Raj? Doesn't he realize this? Does he not have any idea of what he is putting Palak through? Sure, Ishaan said he wasn't doing too well but seriously, there is a really easy solution to it: marry Palak!

'And you know, if he even proposes now, I don't think I am going to say yes. I mean, it would be like he's being forced. I don't want to play that pity card. He should wanna do it on his own. I don't want it to be a compulsion.'

'Okay, I understand. You have a point. It's just hard not to see you two together.'

'Yeah, it is hard for me too,' she laughs bitterly. 'I mean, I never imagined my life without Raj. But now when I think about starting over again, I am not as scared any more. I have to do it. I have no other choice left,' she sighs.

'Hmm . . .' I agree supporting her. She has valid arguments and there is nothing we can do about it.

She has finally entered the world of singledom after so many years. And she is going to have to prepare herself for the many lonely nights to come.

WHATEVER WILL BE, WILL BE

It was Lara's idea to get away. A break from the circus and drama would do us some good. Palak is still engulfed in her own zone and Sanya needs an escape from the city after her big showdown with the bitch of a wife. It had been ages since we last went on a trip, just the four of us, for pure relaxation. And with Palak leaving, it would be a great send off. Our recent trips had been for weddings or big events that usually entailed too much drama, pot and heavy drinking. This time, we intend the weekend to consist only of heavy drinking and smoking.

Sanya is desperate to get out of the city, and she sees no better way of mending an aching heart than with a weekend romp with a hot foreign tourist. She has even opted for a Brazilian wax. Palak isn't functioning normally and had spent the week packing for her move to Hong Kong. Raj's reconciliatory efforts proved to be futile on her.

So we are heading for the beach, sun, cocktails, wine, massages and hot, shirtless men; in short, ultimate bliss! I was super psyched. I hadn't realized how much I yearned for a break until I reached the airport. I was still recovering from the Rajesh blow and looked forward to a break from the city, work and home. Lara is the only one who isn't looking for an escape from reality; she has gracefully accepted her troublesome in-laws.

Since Lara is always meticulous in her planning, we made it her job to organize a perfect last-minute weekend getaway to Goa. With her as the planner we never have to worry about anything; our flights, hotels, pickups and spa appointments are ready and waiting for us. She also carries extra razors, sunscreen, hats and fashion magazines. She's even made prior waxing appointments for us!

When the four of us walk into the airport, any moron can figure out where we are headed! Sanya dressed in her booty shorts clearly broadcasts that we are off for some fun and frolic in Goa. A select few wear shorts on an airplane, that too in India—Sanya is one of them in tiny denim shorts, a pink tank top and wooden bangles. Despite being all smiles, we know she's hurting deeply on the inside.

Lara tries her level best to keep us in the spirit, dressed in full whites, large yellow Chloe bag and yellow flip flops. She is a firm believer of colour therapy: she's dressed Palak up in an orange top and pink flip flops.

I am in a sour mood due to the early morning start at work and the extra work load during the week. My crankiness also stems from the fact that I had been starving myself for a flat stomach for a new blue bikini that Lara insisted I buy, keeping me ravenously hungry at all times. Even my mother kept a watchful eye on me. Last week she slapped my hand away when I reached out for the plate of pakoras at the dinner table.

But Goa's air started to play its dutiful role of lifting our sombre spirits the minute we landed, pumping us up for the weekend. On our car ride to the hotel, the scenic drive through the stretch of coconut and banana trees soothes our nerves and the exciting adventures awaiting us really perks us up. It's the perfect timing for Goa: end November, fewer tourists, good weather and none of the trashy raves.

'I can't wait to hit the bar,' I declare.

'I can't wait to check out the guys,' Sanya chips in.

'I'm gonna clear out the bar,' grins Palak.

Lara smiles happily, 'I knew Goa would do the trick!'

'Let's try and forget the shit we've left behind: the gays, the marrieds, the wusses and the pretentious for a while,' comments Sanya cheekily.

'Oh, I agree!' I nod laughingly.

'And assholes!' laments Palak, punching the air.

We're back on track finally!

But not for long.

Upon entering the hotel the first welcome sign is a large board with 'George weds Anita' written on it.

Palak, Sanya and I turn around and give Lara a horrified look.

'A wedding?' I demand an explanation in disgust.

Lara rolls her eyes, 'Chill, it ends today and they all check out tomorrow morning. It's not the end of the world. Plus, think about it, there will be lots of single young guys to mingle with. Relax now, I booked us a villa.'

'A wedding? Seriously?' I repeat. 'I don't wanna be near anything remotely close to some idiotic thing called lifelong commitment,' I grumble, pissed that it is playing spoilsport to our freshly lifted spirits.

When we walk into our large two-bedroom villa, the soothing, yet opulent décor of whites, creams and mahogany calms me down immediately.

Lara opens up a bottle of tequila in the living room and calls us out, 'Guys, come here.' Pouring out four neat shots for us she toasts, 'We are finally in Goa for a much needed vacation, and we need to loosen up, soak in the sun, leave our worries in Mumbai and have a ball of a time. Palak, a smile!' she orders. 'This is for Hong Kong and for us being friends forever.'

Big smiles ensue and the harshness of the tequila soothes our nerves immediately.

The four of us venture down to the main hotel area in our extra tiny clothes, attracting stares from everyone. There is something about girls on vacation that encourages us to be bold, slut down and bare all! We stroll through a mini courtyard in search of the seaside restaurant and bar promised to us.

I open a large wooden door in anticipation but instead, we stumble into what looks like Anita and George's wedding reception.

The four of us stand there stunned and dressed rather inappropriately for a traditional Christian reception. The venue is breathtakingly beautiful! The guests are crowded around the newly wedded couple, presumably taking their first dance as man and wife; the four of us stop and stare rather rudely at the blushing couple.

Lara whispers, 'That's a Vera Wang.'

I nod in a daze as she points out the virginal flowing, white, strapless floor-length dress with layers of pleated and draped tulle, tiered ruffled skirts, chiffon and lace creating a voluminous effect, with the signature Vera Wang sage green sash below the bust. The bride looks stunningly beautiful with her hair tied back in a loose French knot, laced with delicate diamond studs and pearls.

I take in the grand setting; round tables with pristine white tablecloths, bordered with crochet lace, bouquets of white orchids adorning the centre of the tables and candles exhaling whiffs of light vanilla and jasmine into the love-filled air. The bridesmaids are dressed in pale green satin dresses and the men look dapper in black tuxedos whilst the children run around in wedding finery.

My trained eyes admire every precise detail, every shade of white, cream, green and olive in the decor, flowers, centrepieces and bridesmaids and I start to wonder why I had been reluctant to go into wedding planning. The thought surprises me and the realization that I actually want to marry dawns on me.

It isn't the pangs of worry, stress and pain I usually feel when I'm at these events; the longing for an ex whom I wanted to marry; someone whom I believed I could have had a future with. This time that feeling does not surface. The pain is gone. I feel liberated. I have moved on. Not even for Rajesh. I can't see myself marrying him any more. It's someone else; someone with a little mystery; someone with whom I look forward to waking up every morning and learning something new.

Everything happens for a reason and the fact that I can't picture any of them now makes me happy! I regret nothing, none of my decisions, and savour every moment I have experienced. Smile, Neha, at the good fortune of having let go when you did and with the hope of finding someone better, someone who is actually meant to sweep you off your feet.

I turn to the others beaming, 'Shall we go?'

The three of them nod in stunned unison and follow me out in silence towards the wooden door at the opposite end of the courtyard.

This door leads us to our little piece of heaven: a chic and trendy place by the sea, under a canopy of stars in the Goan nightfall. A live band plays *Volare* in the corner to enhance the lively ambience.

We settle into our table under an umbrella when Lara asks, 'What the hell are you so smiley and happy about? Weren't you the one who was so pissed about the wedding here?'

'Nothing, let's order,' I smile back. I order a pitcher of strawberry margarita, calamari and French fries; eating one normal meal isn't going to affect my bikini body.

'What did you see?' asks an intrigued Sanya.

'I didn't see anything,' I laugh, 'Which is why I am smiling.'

They look at me questioningly.

I clear my throat to explain, 'I was just thinking about how the wedding was so beautiful. And I want one for myself. But I can't picture any particular guy in that scene.'

'So you're going to have a wedding by yourself?' asks Sanya bluntly.

'No idiot, what I mean to say is that I didn't see anyone from my past like I usually do at weddings. I don't regret letting any of those guys exit my life because I can't see them in my future any more when I close my mind and dream of my wedding . . .'

'Ladies, your drinks and food. Can I get you anything else?' asks the waiter while laying down our food.

'Another pitcher of margarita please—we're talking about marriages,' replies Palak dryly as she pours out the stuff into our glasses.

'Certainly,' he smiles.

'Okay, before you talk about your solo wedding, cheers girls, to our Goa trip being fabulous and sexy and of course, to Neha's impending singular marriage,' announces Sanya.

Clinking our glasses in unison, Lara prods me further, 'So you were saying, Neha?'

Gulping down two large sips, I continue, 'I was saying that I can't think of anyone I want to be married to. That none of my exes was the *one* for me. It means when I close my eyes I see someone mysterious and unknown, someone . . .'

'Someone who is tall, around 6 feet?' asks Palak.

'Mmm . . . yes, he's tall,' I try to focus whilst munching on fries.

'Does he have short curly hair?'

'Mmm . . . I don't know that much Palak, why?' I ask annoyed at her disruptive questions. I chow down on some calamari with tartar sauce, still ravenously hungry, suddenly remembering I hadn't eaten anything since my morning toast.

'Could it be Ishaan?' asks Palak.

'Huh?' I ask confused. 'What? No way, he really gets on my nerves. Besides I'm not a model, remember?' I reply instantly. I recall our conversation last week and how his comment had made me wonder, but quickly shake my head to get rid of such ludicrous ideas.

'Does he know you're in Goa?' asks Palak again.

'No, Palak, why are we talking about Ishaan? Can we talk about something more pleasant?'

'Well, he's here.'

'What? Where?'

'Turn around.'

Sanya and I turn around and lo and behold, Ishaan is there at the bar with a few other tuxedo-attired guys.

What the hell?

I yank Sanya around, 'Shush, no need to call him here, it's a girls' weekend remember. And why is he here?'

'He must be here for the wedding which is why he is in a tux,' Lara gushes as if she had just solved the mystery of the Bermuda Triangle. 'Oh and he looks *good*, Neha,' she drools.

'Are you forgetting that he's Ashish's friend?' I retort smugly.

Sanya whines, 'Neha, there's a really cute guy next to him, I want to know who he is, come on, let's go say hi.'

'What? We just turned around for two seconds—how the hell did you see anyone else?'

It's a different issue altogether that I had noticed Ishaan's bowtie loosened around his collar, his sexy smile lighting up the room and a faint pink lipstick mark on his cheek.

How typical of him to hook up with a bridesmaid, and knowing him probably during the wedding too. Grrr . . .

'Neha,' Sanya continues to whine.

'Fine, but let's finish this one drink and the fries first,' I try to buy time to regain my composure.

'Oh you hog, shut up,' and then she yells out waving, 'Yoohoo! Ishaan! Over here!'

I stay put with my back towards him. I hear him approaching and say, 'Hello! What a pleasant surprise, I didn't know you girls were hitting up Goa!'

He slides into a chair next to Palak. He makes eye contact with me and smiles. I ignore him and continue drinking my margarita.

'Okay, dish it, who is that guy who was standing next to you at the bar?'

'Ah, so that's why you called me over? Not so that I can have a drink with you girls or share your fries?' he feigns disappointment, looking directly at me. I, of course, look away again.

Lara starts giggling like an idiot and hands him a dish loaded with food while Palak calls for an extra glass for his margarita. He carefully lifts a fry, dips it in tartar sauce and while chewing, he says, 'That's Keshav from Delhi that you're eyeing. I'll introduce you,' he smiles, his faint dimples glowing in the dim lights.

'I like you, Ishaan,' Sanya smiles sweetly at him and pokes me below the table. I refuse to react, and continue focusing on my calamari rings to line my stomach for more tequila to come throughout the night.

'Actually, why don't we join tables in a bit? It'll be fun!' he suggests.

'Oh yes!' gushes Sanya.

Oh great, what happened to our girls' weekend?

I down the remaining margarita left in my glass and reach out to pour myself another glass. But Ishaan holds back the pitcher and says calmly, 'Neha, it wouldn't hurt to smile you know,' and then drops his voice lower, 'You were smiling ear to ear at the reception. I saw you.' He winks.

'Neha's just moody, especially when she is in the company of really good-looking hunks!' pipes in Sanya, to which I retaliate by throwing my napkin on her.

'Here baby, eat,' pushing forward the plate of fries, still holding back the margarita pitcher. The other girls blatantly exchange conspiring glances, pissing me off even more.

Baby? How dare he!

Sanya cunningly smiles and asks, 'Say, Ishaan, who have you been hooking up with here?' pointing to the lipstick mark on him.

'What?' he asks confused.

Palak raises her eyebrows over her glasses as she presses her finger on his left cheek, 'Pink lipstick!'

He grins sheepishly, 'Nobody. That was my aunt who still thinks I'm an eight-year-old boy!'

I throw him a sceptical look, not buying his story. Unfortunately, he catches my expression.

'What? I'm serious. You don't believe me? I'm going to introduce you to her and you can see the colour of her lips!' he says earnestly, rubbing off his left cheek. 'Let me call the other guys here to join us.'

He gets up and walks towards the bar to call his friends.

Palak waits for him to be out of earshot and then looks at me sternly, 'Neha, why are you so rude to him? He even gave you, and only you, an explanation for the lipstick stain. Did something happen between you two?'

'What? No!'

'Are you sure? I saw him hugging you at Prive.'

'So? It was nothing,' I say defensively.

'They are coming here now, so behave yourself,' Palak warns me.

Ishaan returns to our table and clasps his hands on the back of my chair. To my utmost horror I feel the hair on my back raise as I catch a whiff of his aftershave in the midnight breeze.

'Shall we move to a larger table?' he asks.

'Oh, of course, darling,' chimes Sanya, setting her eyes on Keshav.

Ishaan's friends are super delicious tuxedo-clad men. The three of them, Keshav, Ankit and Neel are typical Delhi brats, 6 feet tall, broad and generously muscular. Impeccably dressed, drool-worthy and absolutely bangable! Sanya is already well settled next to Keshav and starts working her charm. I eye Ankit and Neel, trying to decide which handsome treat I should sit next to since Lara and Palak are thankfully not interested in the game. Neel and I shake hands and he smiles warmly at me. I can't help but blush. He is simply gorgeous!

Maybe he can be my weekend treat? Or maybe more than a treat?

I'm already scribbling 'Neha + Neel 4EVA' in my mind with little hearts draped around.

Wow, how cute! Both our names begin with the letter N! We are definitely destined for each other. Neha and Neel. Neel and Neha. Ooh, I like the sound of that!

Come on, Neha, say something now. Sound smart. Shit, Lara, Sanya, Palak, someone, help me!

'Neha, come here,' booms Ishaan's voice.

No way! Not him!

Ishaan's strong hands grip my shoulders and guide me to a chair next to his. He makes me feel short and a little naked, particularly in my tiny green jumpsuit, while he stands handsomely tall in his tuxedo. And I helplessly look on as Neel and Ishaan exchange glances.

Are you bloody kidding me? What is going on?

I turn and throw a nasty look at Ishaan which he returns with a smile.

Damn it.

The hearts around 'Neha + Neel 4EVA' break one by one and our names slowly fade away.

Neel probably thinks I'm with Ishaan. I AM NOT WITH ISHAAN. I HATE ISHAAN.

The table conversations start off quietly and politely. But as the drinks continue to flow and more food is passed around, our table becomes the loudest by the seaside and our laughter replaces the music. I cannot stop from passing surreptitious glances at Neel every now and then. He removes his jacket to reveal a well-toned body under the fitted shirt, a narrow waist, broad muscular shoulders and a great *tush*! His biceps are almost ripping though his white shirt, making it rather difficult for me to tear my eyes away in my semi-drunken state. I can sense Neel smile back embarrassedly and shift uncomfortably, but for some reason it doesn't affect me.

Ishaan nudges me and leans in closer, 'Stop ogling at Neel. It's really obvious,' he hisses angrily.

I hiss back in his ear, 'What the hell is your problem? He's just sooo hot!' I slur.

'Here, eat some nachos,' an annoyed Ishaan instructs me. 'Slow down on the drinks.'

'Stop acting like Rajesh!' I glare back. Ishaan looks horrified and pours me another glass of margarita in contempt.

'Guys, drinking game?' someone suggests.

'Yes!' I pounce on the idea.

'We can go back to our rooms and hang out there?' proposes Lara.

Sanya and Keshav are almost on top of each other by now.

At our villa, vague images of cards, tequila, some strawberries and a champagne bottle come and go. A few spliffs get passed around and the night plays along in blurry images and laughter and drinks ensue throughout the night, till the wee hours in the morning.

THE MORNING AFTER . . .

The early rays of the sun stream carelessly through the white shades of the windows, forcing my eyes to crack open. I squint my eyes in the light and lift my arm to see the time. Every part of my body aches and screams with pain. The watch says its 8.30 a.m.. I feel a tight belt around me as I let my arm fall back down on the bed. Something warm and hairy.

Oh shit. It's an arm. Not my arm.

An arm that is gently but firmly wrapped around my waist. *Oh shit. Oh shit.*

My half squinting eyes are now wide open. I turn around and Ishaan groggily opens his eyes at me and smiles.

'What—what happened?' I cry frantically.

I push away his arms with force and I raise the sheets to check if my clothing is still on and find both of us fairly dressed—me in my tiny jumpsuit half zipped to my waist and him in just his boxers.

Oh shit! Oh shit! Oh shit!

'Come here, nothing happened, go to sleep, baby,' he gently tries to pull me back down to bed but I don't budge.

'Baby? Baby?' I repeat, aghast and appalled. 'I am *not* your baby. Why are you in my bed?'

'Because you insisted on me taking you to bed. Now come here and go back to sleep.'

'What? How can this happen? You asshole, you think I'm one of your slutty model girlfriends you can just get into bed with? You jerk, asshole, I hate you!' I raise my voice.

'Shhh, Neha, calm down, nothing happened, I promise you. I didn't do anything wrong, we were just really drunk and so we passed out together. Look, Neha, I wouldn't do anything like that with you. So stop pouting and worrying. Come here, and go to sleep.' He stretches his arms towards me and pulls me back towards him. He adds sleepily, 'Now let me hold you and go to sleep.'

I give up, too exhausted and still drunk to argue or fight him off. He hugs me tightly around my bare waist and kisses my forehead. I smile in spite of myself, still in a drunken stupor and drift back to sleepdom.

Ϋ

The strong sun rays filter into the room, making it bright and warm. I stretch out lazily, smiling, having woken up from a nice deep slumber. My eyes half open, I look up to find Ishaan smiling down at me. A scowl replaces my smile.

So much for a beautiful morning.

'What are you looking at?' I grimace, trying to zip up my jumpsuit.

He smiles, amused by my reactions and comments, 'You snore so cutely.'

Yikes!

'Stop smirking, I do not snore. Just go away, I don't want to know what happened.' I toss over and bury my head into a pillow.

'Arrey, Neha, come here, don't think like that, nothing bad happened,' he replies gently, caressing my head.

'Go away,' I muffle from below the pillow.

He tenderly traces my exposed neck, forcing me to turn my head sideways, and he cups my face closer to him.

My bedroom door flings opens and Palak shouts, 'Neha, wake up, we're going to the beach, get rea—oh my God! I'm so sorry, I didn't know!' She stands at the doorway, stunned.

Ishaan sits up and casually says, 'Good morning, Palak.'

'Uhm, good morning,' and she quickly shuts the door firmly behind her.

'I'm going to kill you!' I scream and lunge towards him.

He laughs and catches hold of my arms, pins me back down on the bed and says, 'Look, I like you, and nothing stupid happened last night, okay?'

I lie there breathless and stunned, completely at his mercy, searching for some truth in his eyes. I give up. There's not much I can do with alcohol still in my blood.

I meekly reply, 'Okay.'

'And I think you're beautiful and any guy who is with you will be lucky.'

I look up in shock: *what did we talk about last night? Shit*. I shut my eyes tightly, praying for this to be a bad dream.

Any guy? What does he mean by any guy? Clearly he doesn't intend to be that guy after spending a night with me doing God knows what.

He delicately touches my cheek and asks, 'May I?' My forehead creases up further in anxiety. He kisses my cheek, then the other cheek. I still refuse to open my eyes.

Is this a nightmare?

'Neha!' exclaims Ishaan.

My eyes fly open and I see him staring at me, shocked.

Oops, I said it out aloud.

'You can't blame me, Ishaan. I can't help thinking if this is some kind of disgusting joke you're playing on me. Especially when you're with different girls every night! We are friends, Ishaan, it should be different with me. You should leave me . . .' before I know it, his lips are pressed against mine, my arms pinned down to the bed.

His lips feel soft and supple, and to my own horror, I kiss back. My mind stops thinking and goosebumps conquer my body. The kiss goes on longer than I had expected until he finally breaks away breathless. He looks into my eyes and says gently, 'I'll call you once I'm back in Mumbai, and Monday night I am taking you out to dinner.' He smiles at me, kisses my forehead as I lie there in a daze. 'I leave this afternoon. I'll see you before I go?'

I nod, still stunned.

He is totally in control of this, and I think I like it.

Who would've thought?

He gets up from the bed, while I still lie there mesmerized. As he pulls on his pants and shirt, I can't help but stare at his golden skin gleaming in the sunlight, his well-cut biceps, the athletic shoulders, and the slight beer belly. He is too good to be true. He catches my stare, and I quickly look away, blushing. He slips on his formal shoes, and bends down and gently kisses my lips, cheeks and forehead, before pulling away.

'Bye,' he whispers.

As he walks out the door holding onto his tuxedo jacket, I can only see his tall, broad frame and messy hair. I feel dreamy and in heaven.

Is he the unknown face? No, Neha, don't jump to conclusions.

I let out a huge sigh and lie back in a daze.

'Mmm . . .' I murmur dreamily.

After he leaves, an exponential amount of energy flows through my body and I realize that it has been a while since I smiled so much! Before I can get off the bed, Palak and Lara stumble into the room and drag me out to the living space.

'Oh my God, Neha, what happened?' asks a bewildered Lara. Coffee had already been made for me.

'Nothing happened, we just passed out.'

'And?'

'Mmm . . . we kissed in the morning.'

'That's it?'

'Well, I don't know about last night. I can't remember anything,' I clutch my throbbing head.

'I told you!' exclaims Lara excitedly to Palak, and Palak takes out a 500-rupee note and gives it to Lara.

'What the hell?' I inquire.

'Oh don't worry, I thought you might have done more than that, so I bet a thousand!' says Palak.

'Wow, don't I love you guys!' I laugh.

'Okay, so how was it?' Lara asks excitedly.

'It was . . .' I take my time.

'Come on!'

'Really, really good!' I giggle.

'Where is Sanya?'

'What?' I ask stunned. 'Oh my God, she isn't here?'

'Neha, you don't know?'

'I don't remember anything from last night!'

'Was she with Keshav?'

'Call her.'

Her phone continues to ring with no answer.

'Shit, Neha, call Ishaan, ask for Keshav's number.'

'Hell, no! I am not calling Ishaan!'

'Seriously, come on, for Sanya!' Palak hyperventilates.

'No! You call him. You're his friend too. I am not going to.'

Just then, the main door of our villa buzzes with a key card and Sanya saunters in, smiling brightly despite just having had her walk of shame!

'Good morning, let's go to the pool?' Sanya chirps. And then notices our faces, 'What? What's wrong?'

'Here, let's go to the pool and then talk,' says Lara, handing over Sanya a coffee mug.

Ψ

The four of us lie on the deck chairs in our colourful bikinis with suntan lotions and water bottles and as Sanya reaches out for a magazine, Lara slaps her hand away.

'Dish it first, where were you last night?' commands Lara.

Sanya gives a playful smile, 'Sooo . . . I was with Keshav. We walked along the beach, then I got hungry so he took me to this pizza place close by. Everyone knew him there.' Sanya gets all animated, 'And I really had the best pizza in my life there!' She gushes, 'And then . . .'

'And then what? Hurry up, get to the juicy part,' exclaims Lara.

'And then we went to his room and had some wine . . . and . . . we hooked up!'

'Did you sleep with him?'

'Maybe!' she grins mischievously. 'He's from Delhi, he looks after his father's business. He was engaged once, but broke it off, a year back. And he has been single since then. His ex-fiancée was from London and she's gone back there. So she is definitely out of the picture.'

'Did he say he'll call you?' I ask Sanya.

'Of course he did. And I know he will,' she smiles triumphantly, brimming with confidence.

'Okay, your turn, Neha,' Lara turns to me.

'What? Neha got action?' asks an astonished Sanya.

'Haha, very funny, no action, just a kiss. And he said he'll call me too, and he's going take me out for dinner on Monday,' I retort, playfully indignant.

Lara looks thoughtfully towards me, 'You know, Neha, I think he really does like you.'

'Wait, WHO?' Sanya sits upright in shock.

'Ishaan!' Palak giggles.

'Ishaan? What? This is H-U-G-E! Neha! You and Ishaan? Who on earth would have thought!'

'I don't know, I can't tell,' I reply sombrely, ignoring the giggles.

'Actually, you guys were only talking to each other last night, ignoring everyone else after Palak and Lara went to bed. You were arguing and then laughing, then fighting, then drinking . . . You didn't even notice any of us leave. Sooo . . . I guess it was expected to happen!'

'Well, you're gonna have to fill me in, because I don't remember a damn thing,' I cover my face in remorse.

Sanya continues, 'I mean each time we all meet, he always makes an effort to come up to you and talk to you. At Prive, he only talked to you, he didn't even bother saying hello to us. And he made sure you were okay last night. I mean, he clearly has feelings for you, and getting on your nerves might be his way of proclaiming his undying love for you? Wow Neha, you sure are lucky!' she and Lara laugh.

Palak quietly says, 'Neha, he likes you. I saw the way he was looking at you last night and he was beaming at only you when we bumped into him. Neha, you should give it a thought. He didn't let Neel come near you.'

This is too much for me to handle at this hour, in this heat and with this hangover. I need a drink.

'And Neha, he's Gujarati. His mother is really nice and his whole family is refreshingly *normal*!'Lara stresses. 'He works hard, plays hard; he is perfect. Not to mention how extremely yummy he looks, those dreamy eyes and fit body . . .' Lara trails off.

'Okay, fine, I get it. I need a drink now.'

Palak all if a sudden sits up and says, 'I've made up my mind.'

We all turn to stare at her.

'I'm not going to Hong Kong. In fact, I'm going to leave my job and I want to freelance.' She smiles contentedly—the first real smile we have seen on her since her break up.

We crowd around her to hug her. Our Palak is finally back and she is happy. That's classic Palak. She keeps quiet throughout her 'quarter-life crisis', figures out her feelings, ideas, plans and weighs all the options, pros and cons, and makes her own decision.

She gets up, 'I think I should call Raj now and tell him,' pulls on her cover up and saunters off towards the hotel.

Sanya starts packing up her beach bag, 'Come on, let's go inside and make fun of wedding people.'

Lara and I trail behind a catwalking Sanya, rocking her hips from side to side in her white bikini, catching every man's attention. She is surprisingly awake and alert despite not having slept a wink. I am still woozy, sick and nauseated from last night.

How did all this happen? I used to hate his guts and thought he was excruciatingly annoying. But today, all I can think of is how his strong arms flexed when he pinned me down, how his slight stubble grazed my cheeks, how comforting his bare chest felt against my thin clothes, how he held me so snugly in bed and made me feel so safe and secure . . . Stop. Neha, get a grip.

I look at my phone again but there is still no call or BBM from him.

Maybe my expectations are too high? Maybe he was too drunk in the morning to remember anything. Maybe he didn't like what he saw in the morning? And took the first flight home?

My stomach starts to churn and a sinking feeling forms, either due to anxiety or the hangover. Whatever the reason, the perfect cure would be a Bloody Mary.

'Guys, I really need a drink.'

'Yeah, I'm hungry too, let's eat.'

The packed restaurant is filled with the wedding entourage chattering loudly, including Ishaan having his late breakfast with Ankit and Neel.

Shit! What do I do?

Ishaan immediately gets up from his table and walks over as Lara and Sanya eye him like a hawk to analyse his every movement. He looks good; beige linen pants and loose white linen shirt showing off his golden tanned skin. He is astoundingly scrumptious! He gives me a knowing smile while walking confidently towards me. I feel his eyes bore into mine, reading my thoughts, forcing me to look away.

Ishaan nods at Lara and Sanya and gently takes my hand into his and asks, 'Can I talk to you for a second?'

Sanya promptly replies before I can open my mouth, 'Darling, you can say whatever you want in front of us—we won't make fun of you, I promise,' she smiles teasingly.

I look up to find him staring down at me, waiting for me to say something. I simply cannot resist his sexy smile and his twinkling eyes.

'Let's go.'

'Woot woot,' they catcall as Ishaan places his hand on the small of my back, guiding me out of the restaurant towards the lobby, giving me another set of goosebumps despite the noon heat.

I stick my middle finger out at the girls as we walk out.

'Come, sit. Are you feeling better?' he asks gently, leading me towards the sofa set in the middle of the lobby. I nod, feeling too zoned out to say anything. 'I actually wanted to give you a kiss before I go.'

He cups my face, gently forcing me to look up at him. He gazes into my eyes intently and raises his brows questioningly.

How can I possibly say no to such a hunk? Has he always been this good-looking? Or has the Goan air affected my vision and brain cells?

His touch sends tingles down my body and I pray he never realizes the overwhelming effect he has on me.

'Neha?' His voice jerks me out of my trance. I smile, nodding.

He leans forward and I shut my eyes only to feel a kiss on my forehead.

'I am leaving in an hour so I'll see you on Monday. And I'll call you tomorrow night once you're back in town. Enjoy the rest of the weekend, and please don't fall asleep with anyone else,' he laughs jokingly.

'What the . . . Shut up,' I retort and playfully stretch out to whack him. But he catches my hand and pulls me forward into a hug. I succumb into his arms and hug back. I realize that I am going to miss him tonight and start wishing that he could stay on.

Oh man, I am so falling for this hottie!

'Come on, let's get you something to eat,' and he leads me back towards the restaurant holding my hand lightly.

What is it about him that makes my whole body tingle? He makes me feel comfortable, yet keeps me on the edge; a rather strange feeling but an exciting one nonetheless.

When we return to the restaurant, Sanya and Lara already

have their attention glued to the door, waiting for us. Their
eyes fixate on our joined hands.

Ishaan looks at me, gives me his heart-melting smile and
whispers, 'See you in Mumbai and you take care.' He leans
down to my short frame to kiss my head and gently ruffles my
hair as we approach my table. He bids goodbye to my friends,
winks at me and walks away.

I turn to Lara and Sanya, beaming.

'What?' I ask innocently.

'Neha? Are you already dating?' exclaims Sanya.

'Well, I don't know, but he just wanted to tell me that he
was leaving now and he will call me tomorrow night and that
he's going to take me out on Monday night. Oh and he kissed
me on my forehead.'

Lara gasps, 'Guys only kiss girls on the forehead if they are
in love with the girl. Neha! He really loves you! I think Neha
is going to marry soon!' she singsongs.

'Hold on, let's take it easy. I don't know yet what's going
to happen, what's going on or whether he's gonna call or not,'
I say doubtfully.

Sanya calmly advises, 'Neha, just go with the flow. You never
know what can happen. I know it's a little unnerving at first,
but it may just turn out to be really good.' She reaches out to
pat my hand with a reassuring smile and resumes buttering
her toast.

'Hmm, I need to eat now.'

The three of us chatter, gossip and laugh and more
importantly, gorge on the lavishly laid out buffet, eating
everything from waffles, pancakes, croissants, eggs and bacon.
I have another coffee before starting with mimosas.

Watching me, Sanya comments, 'You know Neha, you
aren't dating as yet; you still need to watch your waistline!'

Palak walks in, smiling brightly as she seats herself down and begins, 'I'm sorry I know this is supposed to be an all-girls weekend, but Raj really wants to come down. Is that okay?' She looks at us enquiringly.

'Oh of course Palak, you don't need to ask. You deserve to spend the night with him instead of us, especially now that you aren't going away!' We all nod and gush in delight.

She thanks us profusely and promptly picks up her BlackBerry to call Raj and says, 'Come here, baby, as fast you can.' She looks over at Lara and adds, 'Inform Ashish that you're coming and see if he can come with you.'

Lara instantly perks up and gulps down her mimosa.

'This has been such a good, unexpected trip so far!' gushes Sanya dreamily.

'What did I miss?' asks Palak.

'Ishaan came back to say bye to Neha and kissed her on the forehead. They're going on a date on Monday,' reports Sanya.

'What?' exclaims a wide-eyed Palak.

Oh man.

Before anyone can go on further, I head back to the buffet table to reassure myself with another chocolate croissant.

THE BEACH AND OUR BOYS

After a lazy snooze on the beach and a mouth-watering late afternoon Goanese lunch of peri peri lobster, jumbo prawns, fish curry and rice accompanied with many cocktails, Raj and Ashish arrive at the hotel, lifting Palak and Lara's spirits to new highs.

Palak runs into Raj's arms like a dramatic *Dilwale Dulhaniye Le Jayenge* scene. They both burst out in tears in the lobby as they hold each other, hugging and kissing incessantly.

'I'm sorry, I'm really sorry,' Raj repeats while hugging her relentlessly.

'I love you and I am so sorry,' Palak says in between kisses.

It became one of the most romantic scenes I have ever seen in real life!

While the two couples go off on their own, Sanya and I laze by the poolside with magazines and mojitos in the evening breeze. The hotel had thankfully quietened down since the wedding party left!

Beep. Ishaan: 'Hi baby, I've reached home. I hope you're having a good time. Thinking of you. HUG.'

I reply: 'Hi. Yes I am. ☺'

'That's a bit cold, isn't it?' Sanya points out.

'What?' I see Sanya peering through her oversized sunglasses into my phone.

'Send another BBM with a hug emoticon,' she instructs.

'Excuse me, do you mind?' I move away but send the hug to him anyways.

She does have a point.

'Sooo . . . you and Ishaan? I think I can see the future with you two in it!'

'Sanya! Stop it. I don't want to think about it.'

Please don't jinx us.

'Had you ever thought about Ishaan in this way before? I mean did you ever have feelings for him?'

No, I never did. And I am shit scared to think about it even now.

'I don't know, it's quite confusing. And Ishaan has never been serious about any girl. And maybe it's just Goa making us behave like this,' I laugh it. 'I have a feeling that as soon as we meet in Mumbai, everything is going to be normal again.'

I hope not. I hope he really meant what he said. And I hope he doesn't change his mind. I hope it never becomes normal. I like this feeling.

'Really? Is that what you think?'

'Yep,' I try to sound truthful.

No.

'And are you okay with that?'

Hell no. But I have to be prepared, right?

'Yeah, of course. I mean I can't keep any expectations from Ishaan. It's Ishaan after all! And it would be stupid of me to believe that there will be anything more to this after just a weekend.'

Please Ishaan, don't hurt me.

'Neha, I really don't think that is the case with him. I think he is looking for something more than just a weekend. You better tell him if you feel otherwise. But something tells me that you are just putting on a face and that you are actually hoping for more.'

I remain silent.

Sanya persists, 'Neha! Tell me what's on your mind. You cannot screw this up because of some random shit in your dumb head.'

'Okay, fine. I really don't want to keep my hopes high on Ishaan because he is a friend first and I don't want to screw it up. And also, I don't know how I feel about being in a relationship. I never got them right before, like you said I don't want to screw it up, especially not with Ishaan. He is special . . . kinda . . .'

'You like him! And if you are so worried about screwing it up, it means you really do care about him, and all the more reason you should give it a shot. It's too late to worry about the friendship aspect because you have already swapped spit!' she smiles mischievously.

'I guess . . .' I trail off, preferring to sip on my mojito, my eyes squinting in the sun.

'Neha, why don't you just wear sunglasses?'

'No way! It makes my nose look weirder.'

'Fine!' Sanya shakes her head, 'Back to Ishaan, please.'

'I do not want to think of marriage or anything. I just want to go with the flow. I don't want to think. I just want things to take their own course. If it's meant to be, it will be.'

'Okay, that's a good outlook. So tell me, is he a really good kisser?'

'Sanya!' I blush.

'Come on, you know we all drool over him!' she giggles.

'Okay, enough about Ishaan. Tell me about Keshav.'

Sanya groans, 'I don't know. I am not ready for anything serious yet. He seems like a nice guy. But I'm really not interested.

I think I need to be alone for a while. Learn to be by myself. I have always been seeing someone or counting on someone to hold on to. I think it's time to hold on to myself.'

'Really?'

'Yeah. I'm gonna need some time to get Sanjay out of my system. Though catching him red-handed with Monica the other day definitely did help speed up my recovery process!' she laughs. 'How many concubines must he have? I feel so grossed out! And really, really used! I always believed he never said he loved me because he felt guilty or tried to . . . I don't even know!' her voice chokes. She wipes a tear under her sunglasses. 'Ugh!' Sanya smiles bravely, 'Not everyone is like that and I have no one but myself to blame!'

'Well, that's true,' I am honest. 'But like you said, love arrives at the most unexpected hour!'

'Hmm . . . let's drink to that! For unexpected love! Especially you and Ishaan!' she laughs.

'I wish he had stayed tonight,' I comment.

Ύ

Saturday night in Goa proves to be even more eventful than Friday night.

After sunset Palak bounces back into the villa, her face shining with glee.

'We're engaged!' she screams at the top of her voice while jumping up and down.

Squeals of delight ensue and we all rush to see her sparkling ring. Her face emanates a warm and contented radiance. I had never seen her so happy before.

'Everything is becoming all right!' she declares with tears in her eyes. 'Just yesterday everything was crumbling apart.'

We gather into a tight group hug.

'I can't believe I almost gave up on him,' Palak cries.

'I think it's time to celebrate!' Sanya laughs with joy.

'Raj booked us a table at some Italian place, let's get ready.'

'Neha, you're phone is buzzing non-stop! Is it Ishaan BBMing you?' coos Lara.

It is.

Ishaan: 'Hi sweetie . What are you doing? I really wish I could have stayed one more night.'

I reply: 'Hey! Was lazing by the poolside. What are you up to?'

Ishaan: 'I was hoping for a I miss you reply, but it's okay. LOL. I have to finish off some work and probably go out for a drink later.'

I reply: 'Any hot date tonight?'

Ishaan: 'My hot date is in Goa right now, so will be going solo tonight.'

I sigh with relief. Maybe he is serious after all.

I reply: 'Is she just a date for a few nights?'

Ishaan: 'I hope not. I would like it to be for a very long time.'

I smile wider, my heart racing faster.

I reply: '☺'

I don't quite know what else to say.

Ɏ

We settle down in the rather posh Italian restaurant, a charming colonial cottage, set amidst luscious gardens overlooking the Baga River. A comforting warmth exudes from the dim lights and a faint breeze carries the sounds of soft jazz to our tables, creating a sanctuary away from the world. Palak's vibrant, excited and giggly mood hasn't subsided yet.

'So how did Raj propose?'

'Well, he filled our room with flowers and candles. There was a bottle of champagne chilling in a bucket, a plate of chocolate-dipped strawberries and he even brought fresh macaroons from Toujours. He actually carried them in his hand on the flight!' Palak gushes. Raj continues to pick on a bread roll, blushing in embarrassment.

Palak goes on, 'He blindfolded me when he took me up to the room! And when I opened my eyes, I was so shocked! He managed to coordinate all that in such a short time!'

Raj has never been known to be the romantic kind so this story is rather surprising and amusing to all of us.

Palak hasn't touched her Carpaccio yet, 'And then he got down on one knee and asked me to marry him!' her eyes sparkle in the candlelight even more than her three carat diamond engagement ring. *Oohs* and *aahs* ensue as she beams away to glory, squeezing Raj's hands.

Lara and Ashish canoodle each other in their corner; them being romantic is quite usual but Palak and Raj have never been big fans of PDA. Sanya and I smile at each other. It has been a pleasant turn of events, something we all desperately needed. It gives us hope that everything can be all right; that new beginnings are always around the corner.

'So I hear there's a new couple on the rise?' Ashish raises his eyebrows towards me while the others exchange conspiring glances. The girls start giggling; I blush.

'Is that who you have been messaging incessantly since we got to dinner?' asks Raj. 'Even through my very romantic proposal story?' He pretends to be offended.

'Yes, she is! I've been eavesdropping on her texts!' smirks Sanya.

'Who would've thought?' wonders Raj thoughtfully.

'Actually, I'm really happy. Hopefully, now Lara will stop drooling all over Ishaan. I think she'll have more respect for her friend's boyfriend than her fiancé's friend!' Ashish teases.

Lara playfully rubs his belly, 'You know I only have eyes for you!'

'Yeah, right!' Ashish rolls his eyes. 'Maybe once I build my arms and reduce the paunch in time for our wedding,' he pats his belly proudly.

'Oh come on, you know I love your stomach!' she giggles as she tickles his belly.

As the two cooing couples indulge in romance, Sanya and I pick on the salad and bruschetta.

Shall I message Ishaan again? No, maybe it is too soon. And maybe he is on a date right now. Back to models after short and deformed Neha. Hmpf! No forget it. He isn't worth it. I am worrying myself for nothing. I was just a Goa fling for him!

Sanya interrupts my thoughts, 'Message him since you so want to!'

'I don't want to,' I insist.

I hate being so transparent to my friends. What is going on? How did all this happen? Are all hook ups like this for him? I rarely see him with the same girl twice so maybe it's the same thing with me. I mean why on earth would I be an exception? I look nothing like a model for one thing! And I have never been an exception in my life before! Maybe I should just message him and say, what happened was wrong and we should just continue to be friends and pretend like nothing ever happened. He shouldn't feel like he owes me anything just because we are friends. Because he doesn't. And I don't either. I don't even know if I want to owe him anything. There has to be some explanation. Damn it! Why does the weirdest shit always happen to me?

I do the only thing that can keep me from doing anything stupid: switch my phone off.

'Coward!' hisses Sanya.

'Jesus, are you always this nosy?'

'Everything you do is my business,' she grins. 'Or else you would be left nowhere with that loser attitude of yours!'

I switch my phone back on, refusing to be called a coward or a loser.

What if things get screwed up between us? It would be so weird. Oh my God, what if we break up and then start dating other people. Okay, more like I will have to see him with the hottest model while I will still be playing third leg to either Palak and Raj or Lara and Ashish! No, this is way too much of a risk to take. Nothing good can come out of friends starting to date. It just doesn't work! Especially with someone like Ishaan.

I message him: 'Hi. Look, do not worry about last night. You should go ahead with whatever you want. I hope we can continue to be friends, there are no hard feelings. We'll pretend as if nothing happened! ☺'

I wait with my heart in my mouth for a response. The Delivered tick mark on the BBM chat window turns 'R' for read.

Now wait for him say, 'Phew! I think so too! It was a big mistake.'

The clock continues ticking, and he still doesn't reply. I continue nibbling on the Carpaccio.

Twenty minutes pass and still no response.

Shit. What did I do? No, Neha, you did the right thing. He was probably too scared to say it himself.

Twenty-four minutes later his reply arrives: 'If that's what you'd like.'

Whoa! Cold, crude and bitchy! Why is he putting it in my hands?

Beep. Tanya from work: 'Urgent meeting at 9.15 a.m. on Monday. Make sure you're on time.

Crap! I hate work. And now I have lost my appetite. I think I should just stick to the wine.

Wood-fired pizzas appear to change my mind and I dig into the cheesy basil delight for some temporary joy and to forget about Ishaan. But the effort proves to be futile. Ishaan still persists in every corner of my brain.

What the hell is wrong with me? I have never been like this. Food always does the job.

Dessert arrives, the restaurants famed chocolate soufflé and lots of champagne, to celebrate Palak and Raj's engagement. I indulge in hopes of momentary comfort but without any luck.

IN THE END WE ONLY REGRET THE CHANCES WE DIDN'T TAKE

My phone rings on the way to work early Monday morning. It's Ishaan. Since the last cold-hearted message there had been no contact whatsoever. I hadn't bothered to reply.

'Hello?'

'Hi,' he sounds uncertain.

'Hi.'

'How are you?'

'Fine.'

'Did you sleep well?'

'Yup.'

'So, can I see you for dinner tonight?'

I pause.

'Neha?'

I don't respond.

'Neha, look, I just want to talk about what happened.'

'Nothing happened.'

'Yes, it did happen. How can you just throw it out of the window like that?'

'I learnt from you.'

179

'Neha! Just see me tonight.'

'Fine!' I grumble.

'Where do you want to go?'

'I don't care.'

'Olive?'

'Okay.'

'All right, I'll pick you up around 9 p.m.?'

'Okay.'

'Okay, see you tonight. Have a good day.'

Holy crap. Neha. What is wrong with you? Why can't you talk normally? It's just Ishaan. He is your friend. It's just like going out with Sanya, Lara or Palak. Keep it together. It's just dinner. Think about food. Think Italian and wine . . . okay, stop. It's going to be a wonderful day. And everything is going to be just fine.

Beep. Ishaan: 'I am just as nervous as you are. But I can't wait to see you tonight. Hug.'

I smile in amazement.

This is actually happening? Ugh, why can't I get rid of the nervousness and excitement. The butterflies are having a field day in my tummy.

I reply: 'Me too. I'm sorry I was rude. ☺'

Ishaan: 'Don't be sorry, just see me tonight.'

🍸

Getting back to work on Monday morning is a nightmare. Tanya warns me that Monica had been a terror throughout the weekend, getting everyone to work while she snoozed away.

'She made us all come in by 9 on Saturday morning and didn't turn up till two in the afternoon!'

'Oh shit, are you serious?'

'Yeah! And she wanted to see the drafts of some of the new literature we were finalizing before they went to print. But because she was late we couldn't get them to the printers on time. And she wanted them by today morning, but who on earth is going to work on Sunday? Even when she came in, had she immediately read through them we could have made it on time, but she didn't and then of course, she pores over every word and punctuation so it took her till night to approve them! And she is really pissed off now and has been throwing humongous tantrums.'

'Ugh, can I quit?' I ask, not ready to face Monica today.

'Is that a hickey on your neck?'

'What?' I freeze in shock.

Tanya bursts out laughing, 'You better cover that up.'

Shit, how the hell did I get a love bite? So something did happen at night, which I don't remember. I'm gonna kill him. How come my mum didn't notice? Or Sanya, Lara or Palak?

'Where is it?'

'Nowhere,' she shrugs carelessly, 'I was just trying to confirm if you hooked up with someone in Goa! And you did! Come on, dish it, who was it?' Tanya giggles.

'Tanya!' I heave a sigh of relief. 'This kind of shock first thing in the morning was not needed!'

The 9.15 a.m. meeting starts at noon thanks to Monica's tardiness. She chairs the meeting with her big breasts spilling onto the table while Harry darling sulks like a loser on the side. The last momentous PR strategy we played out proved to be a success and share prices had recovered. But clearly she wants something more. I still don't understand the urgency of this meeting.

'Monica would like to completely revamp her and her

company's image,' announces Rita. 'Too much bad press has affected their public face. We need more philanthropy, social work, humanitarian gestures etcetera, etcetera, you get the gist,' she drones on.

Even Rita looks like she is fed up of her biggest clients and lover boy.

Monica starts yapping, 'I just saw the campaigns of Karuna Real Estate which is run by Peter & Co. They have put that bitch Karuna everywhere in their campaign and look at the ghastly job they have done.'

Karuna, considered a big media whore, is Monica's arch rival in the society circle; her family owns Karuna Real Estate Company. She is Monica's nemesis when it comes to grabbing attention, with an equally hideous Botoxed and silicone-injected body but with a lot more cash and diamonds dripping off her.

'I want the same thing,' Monica continues. 'She doesn't even have a degree so how can they make her the face of the company? Well two can play the game,' she declares vehemently.

Monica continues with her tantrums and demands for an hour until we all tune out. My scribbling pad becomes a mass of doodles, stick drawings and lines.

The occasional dreams of Ishaan's arms, biceps, stubble and eyes keep interrupting my attempts to work. I just want the day to end as soon as possible and see Ishaan. I cannot remember the last time I longed to see someone so impatiently. Maybe things are just about to get better.

But nothing of the sort will happen tonight. We are just two friends. It's diplomatic Ishaan after all! He probably just wants us to end on a good note. Wait. Us? There is no 'us'! And there never shall be an 'us'.

Before I leave for home, Rita calls me into her cabin.

'Did you want the application form for the job posting?'

'Umm, yeah sure,'

'Tanya is going to apply for the position as well. I suggest you take this seriously, Neha.'

'Yes, I will,' I politely reply as Rita hands me the application paper.

I can't possibly be thinking of more responsibility when I have Ishaan on my head.

🍸

While I get ready for dinner, a queasy knot forms in my stomach.

Neha, it's just Ishaan. Just a casual dinner and nothing else. It is not a date.

But I still dress up; skinny jeans and a flattering maroon top.

Might as well make him feel like he lost out on something!

I apply some blush-on and mascara and I tousle my hair gently with mousse to give it some natural looking volume. He shouldn't think I made a big effort for him.

I wait in the building foyer as he pulls up in the driveway. When our eyes meet I realize what a big mistake I'm making.

I shouldn't have agreed to this. I can't even face him. Shit, shit, shit, shit . . .

I stand still in front of the passenger door, fiddling with my purse. Ishaan gets out from the car and comes over.

'Get in the car, Neha,' he says softly.

I take a deep breath.

'Neha, we'll drive around and talk. Then you can decide if you want to go eat or not.'

I nod and he opens the door for me.

Why am I giving him such a hard time? Why am I giving myself such a hard time?

As he drives down Alta Mount Road, we maintain a tense silence. A rather uncomfortable one. We pass the building where we caught Monica red-handed with Sanjay; it doesn't bring a cheeky smile to my face right now.

'What are we doing?' I break the silence.

'Well, I thought everything was going smoothly until you decided to forget everything,' he starts. 'Neha, I am not going to be able to forget this. I didn't intend any of this to happen, nor had I ever imagined that I would start having such feelings for you. But it has happened and I think for a reason.'

I keep silent trying to digest everything he is saying.

Ishaan? Feel?

'So what you are saying is that Friday night wasn't just a random hook up for you?'

'No, Neha! Why is it so hard for you to understand? I wouldn't say all these things to you if I didn't mean it. I am not a jerk as much as you'd like to believe that! And it's you, Neha. You're not some random girl. You are Neha, one of my friends and I would never take such a risk with you.'

I still don't have the courage to say anything to him.

'I need to know how you feel,' he asks slowly, almost as if he were scared to find out.

'I don't know. I mean, I'd like to believe everything you say. I haven't felt like this in a while, and I think I'm still trying to recover from Friday night.'

'Neha, I think you're quite special,' he says softly. 'I'd never hurt you intentionally. I think if we give us a shot, it may work out to be great.'

Us.

'I think we can give it a shot,' I whisper.

'Really?' Ishaan's spirits lift up again.

I bite my lower lip, trying not to smile too much. He stops the car by the kerbside and reaches over to hug me.

'I promise I will give us a hundred and fifty per cent,' he blurts out.

'I still cannot get over the fact that you and I happened,' I sheepishly say.

'Neither can I! And I never dreamt of being on a date with you.'

'Excuse me? What does that mean?'

'I mean I never thought that a day like this would come. I have always been fond of you, Neha, but I didn't think anything would ever happen between us, because . . .'

'Because you're always distracted by models!'

'Oh, are you saying that you always wanted something with me, but you didn't because of them?'

'No!' I say, getting flustered. 'I mean . . . What I mean is don't make up stories. I don't think you ever liked me like this before!'

'Okay, I will admit, I never thought about you like that before. But that day when you entered with that wimp at Aer and I saw him touching you, I felt something. I didn't really like it.'

'What? Why? You mean to say you didn't like Rajesh?'

'Oh please, I don't want to hear his name! I could tell you were really making an effort and it affected me to see you sad. And it really pissed me off when I saw you at the bar and he kissed you,' Ishaan fumes. 'And I got even more annoyed when you told me to stop behaving like Rajesh in Goa. If I had stopped you from drinking so much then perhaps you may have remembered some of the night!'

I am dumbfounded.

Ishaan feels like this?

'And I kept asking myself, why does what happens in your life bother me so much? And in Goa, when I saw you eyeing Neel, I flipped. I did not want you anywhere near him. I am sorry, but I was being selfish. Because, if something happened between you two, I would have died! So I kind of indicated to him to back off, because you were mine,' he grumbles.

I gasp. 'I knew you had something to do with that!' my eyes fly wide open.

'Oh, I'm sorry, would you rather be at dinner with Neel right now?' he looks seriously offended.

'What? No! Ishaan!'

'Are you sure? Was I a one-night thing for you? A little holiday?' Ishaan worries.

'Are you kidding me, Ishaan? No, of course not!' I exclaim.

'I hope not,' he replies sheepishly. 'I like you, Neha. And I am hoping this works out. And I am being one hundred per cent serious. This isn't a fling for me.'

'Ishaan, it isn't for me either. I'm just a little overwhelmed and I'm finding this really hard to believe and digest. This is new for me. And I don't know what to expect. And I don't want to have any expectations, because I know I'm not your usual type. Maybe you are experimenting for all I know! I am kind of scared if things go awry. I mean, we are friends first.'

'Believe me; I am just as terrified as you. And please do not say that you are not my type. You are a girl. I like girls! And I do value our friendship and if the Goa incident had not happened, I don't know if we would ever have reached this stage, because I would be too scared to approach you,' he explains. 'And I know you never would have. I honestly think you noticed me only because I steered you away from Neel,' he grumbles.

I cannot help but laugh as his face scrunches up in anxiety. I reach over and place my hand over his. 'Ishaan, relax. I think everything happens for a reason. And let's just see how this goes.'

'But you cannot see anyone else,' he protests.

I laugh, 'Of course not! But does that mean we are dating exclusively?'

'Yes, Neha! I am not sharing you with anyone else and I don't like all these fancy words. You're my girl. And that's it,' he says stubbornly.

And I have absolutely no complaints!

I smile, 'I am yours,' I say quietly.

'Now, can we go eat? Spicy linguini with prawns?'

I smile even wider, 'Yes!'

The advantages of dating a friend: they already know what you order.

'And please, no wine. I know that prick made you drink a lot of wine,' Ishaan says with disdain. 'We'll have champagne. I think we ought to celebrate,' he winks, as he heads towards Olive at the Race Course.

Dinner turns out to be one of the most relaxed yet exciting dates I have ever been on. No wonder he has girls fawning over him all the time.

'Now that I think of it, have you ever had a real girlfriend before? As in, an actual one whom you were committed to?' I ask between bites of my crab cake.

'Well, not really. I actually don't have time or energy to give in a relationship. Plus, my work takes up all my time. I really didn't want to be sparing whatever time I had on a relationship.'

I raise my eyebrows.

'That was then,' he quickly adds, realizing how wrong that sounded.

Ever since I have known Ishaan, he has never had a serious relationship.

'And now?'

'Now things have changed. I am settled, focused and I have you. I don't mean to sound overwhelming, but I always knew that if I ever got into a relationship it would be with someone I really do want to be committed to, not with someone with whom I think I may want to be committed to. I know you and appreciate you already. I wanna take care of you. And now that I think of it, I'm really surprised how you aren't attached to anyone.'

'I don't think anyone thinks like you do,' I reply wryly. I gently touch my nose.

'Oye, shut up! And eat properly. We'll share a tiramisu later.'

On the drive back, Ishaan holds my hand all the way till my building. He leans over to hug me and kisses me on the forehead. Not on the lips. Just the forehead.

'Goodnight. I will call you later.'

I nod, blushing, and get out of the car.

Y

I call Lara since she is the only one who would be able to hear my love shit right now.

'He kissed me on the forehead.'

'Oh my God! That means he loves you! Has he said it yet?'

'No, Lara. We are just dating now. Nothing more.'

'This is really, really exciting, Neha! I mean, I really think this is it for you!' Lara starts singing like a fool, 'Neha and Ishaan, sitting on a tree! K-I-S-S-I-N-G!'

'He didn't kiss me on the lips though. Isn't that weird?' I ponder.

'No, Neha! Not at all. It's his way of saying he isn't just looking to get laid. And might I add that's some real self-control for Ishaan!' she laughs. 'Ooh . . . you are so lucky, Neha!' she giggles.

Oh boy!

LIFE IS FULL OF SURPRISES

We thought we had just about all the excitement we could take during the Goa weekend. We thought wrong. The month of December churned out life-changing moments, surprises and new experiences for us.

Palak quit her job the following Monday after Goa. Her next full-time assignment is planning her official engagement ceremony as well as become further involved in my personal life, that is Ishaan. She wants to know every single detail, analyse every message, intercept every conversation and make her own judgements and predictions. She also counsels Sanya and takes her out every day—they spend hours discussing my relationship with Ishaan among other topics like Sanjay, Lara's in-laws and engagement party planning.

Ishaan and I have spent quite a few very enjoyable hours together. Romantic dinners, quick lunches, occasional coffee breaks from work and the best, late night drives! The moonlight drives are the best because I can actually hold his hand and get touchy-feely with him. It has rapidly become clear that we aren't just casually dating any more. There is much more to this relationship. And that fact is still taking me time to digest.

He is my boyfriend! I have a boyfriend! And I am his girl.

It's a euphoric feeling. The kind that makes you smile randomly when tackling mundane tasks. Despite facing hell at work, the sight of Ishaan makes everything okay, and though Ishaan's work hours are erratic, he makes the time for me, even if it is just for a quick mid-afternoon coffee and a kiss. Within the month, our relationship has blossomed to new heights. And I haven't run yet. Nor am I feeling suffocated. For the time being, life is great.

On Saturday night we decide to meet for drinks at Tote. And since the four of us had not met together since Goa, we ask our respective boyfriends to join us later. Boyfriends . . . *blush!*

Lara bounces in late, fully charged up.

'Guess what?' She glows like a 120-watt light bulb. I pass her a tequila sunrise cocktail while she settles down excitedly.

'What?' I ask in between sips of my tequila cocktail.

'Ashish gave me the surprise of my life! Something even more shocking and unexpected than his proposal!' she beams mysteriously at our clueless expressions.

'We are buying our own separate home!' she shouts over the music with utter joy.

'Oh my God! That is the best news ever! How did it all happen?' Sanya shrieks.

'Well, I don't know exactly, but I always wanted our own place because, you know, his mother and sisters and I never get along,' Lara rolls her eyes. 'So I did suggest casually a long time back that maybe if we lived separately, there might be some peace in the house. So Ashish apparently had been hunting for a place for quite some time and trying to get his parents to agree. They hated me even more! Because as expected, they started to conspire among themselves that I was taking him away from them. So they told him that they have a flat in the suburbs, and that we should live there. I was like, no fucking way! I am from SoBo and I will never cross the border. My boutique is here, my family, my work, everything is here. And more importantly, Ashish's work is also here! It will be hell for him to commute.'

'Ew! The suburbs?' scorns Sanya. 'Oh please, Lara, I cannot imagine you in those filmi avatars! Sequins will replace everything you own! No way!' Sanya crinkles her nose in distaste as she calls for another round of drinks. Sanya is a hardcore townie!

'Yeah, I know!' Lara rolls her eyes. 'So I had given up all hope and accepted that if I wanna be with Ashish, I'm gonna have to live with the monsters. I never brought it up again. But I guess the whole engagement party nonsense must have made Ashish think again. And although he never said anything to me, he must have given his parents an earful,' she smiles as her eyes begin to get wet. 'They sold that flat and bought one on Peddar Road for us! Now we are both close to work, our families and things just can't get any better. His mother still doesn't talk to me, but his sisters have opened up. So I guess it's almost a win-win situation,' she shrugs with relief. 'And they have agreed to let me design their outfits with more suitable colours!' she laughs amusedly.

'Wow! We're glad it finally happened. It will just be a matter of time now before everything else becomes fine,' says Palak.

'Yeah! Finally my patience and perseverance has paid off. I had almost given up on having a peaceful relationship with his family, but now I feel so relieved and even happy,' she smiles widely. A wave of contentment passes over her. She is finally relaxed and at peace.

'Finally, things are getting better!' I gush. We spend a moment in a happy silence.

As an afterthought, Lara adds matter-of-factly, 'Well his mum's still a cow!' We burst out laughing and we clink our drinks to that.

'But at least I don't have to wake up every day and see her face,' she points out. 'And no one will have to hear or get involved in our hostility. We just have to wait for his sisters to marry and find their own kind of guys whom the parents will approve of!'

'Ohhh,' I laugh loudly, 'but who on earth will marry the sisters?' My third cocktail is already giving me a good buzz.

'Well, at least they'll get better guys than Reema, Mona and Reshma,' Sanya grins evilly.

'Maybe, but they will definitely only be allowed to marry within the Marwari caste. I think one outcast in the family is more than enough for them to handle. And honestly, I don't want anyone else to ever face the same problems that I did. My love metre is really high so I can bear it! I doubt anyone else can handle it the way I did.'

'Oh dude, I heard Reema is dating someone!' divulges Palak, our gossip queen.

'Whoa! Whom? Who on earth is so blind?' I respond instantly.

'She is actually dating some thirty-five-year-old banker. He's a divorcee. I don't know many details but, you know, it's big news if a man is voluntarily dating that *thing*,' Palak smirks. 'I think the parents are also involved if I'm not mistaken. So maybe it is an arranged thing!'

'Well, I guess God really has made someone for everyone!' Sanya laughs amusedly.

'Does Mona know about you and Ishaan?' asks Lara.

'Oh man! I have no idea!' I say.

'Everyone knows about Neha and Ishaan!' giggles Palak.

'It's really big news. And just so you know, Mona is not very happy about it! I hear she is fuming.'

'Damn, why do those bitches always have their claws on us?'

'No honey, they may have their claws on you, but not on me!' winks Lara. 'They can't come anywhere near me or Ashish,' she says teasingly.

'They can't do anything to you, Neha!' says an exasperated Sanya. 'Stop being so fearful all the time. No one can prick you without your permission.'

'Ohh . . . wait, I have to show you guys my engagement card!' Palak gushes. 'Sanya and I have spent so much time on this and it has turned out just as I wished!'

She hands out three lavender-coloured envelopes embossed with gold designs. Inside is a rectangular handmade paper card, in matching shades. The elegant, traditionally English-styled invite has an embossed Victorian foil border in gold against the pale lavender background and a bouquet of starburst lilies pressed on the lower right side. The text in curvy black font reads:

Dear Family & Friends,

We are excited to announce our engagement and invite you to be a part of the celebrations for our official ring ceremony and dinner on Sunday, 9 January 2012, at 6 o'clock in the evening, at Regal Room, Trident Oberoi, Mumbai.

Warm regards,
Palak & Raj

'It's so elegant and sophisticated!' I say appreciatively.

'Yeah, I assumed since it is just a ring ceremony I can do without any Indian motifs. So the Victorian-themed engagement party. Then for the wedding we can have everything traditionally Indian,' explains Palak.

Sanya is smiling again and seems to be doing pretty okay despite refraining from her usual hectic social calendar since her public showdown. She hadn't been attending any of her NGO meetings, fundraisers or charity events. Having Palak around her all the time seems to have distracted her from moving into an isolated shell after the humiliation—helping Palak is quite a job since she is a serious task master!

Palak brings it up, 'Neha, what happened about the promotion offer?'

'Huh?'

'Did you apply for the position?'

'Oh, Rita spoke to me last week about it again. The applications have started and she gave me a form too.'

'And?'

'I'm still thinking about it.'

'Neha, are you serious?' Sanya comments quietly.

I look at her surprised. Sanya never takes work or her various careers seriously.

'Well, you are in a rut. You're in a job which you hate sometimes and show no enthusiasm for it. You are being offered a promotion and you just don't care! You're basically letting the promotion go, Neha! Don't you think you need to step it up a bit?'

'Wait, where is this coming from?' I ask, bewildered.

'Neha, you have been in the same position for the last three years—do you not think you should be trying to achieve some sense of fulfilment now?' asks Palak.

'But why does it matter? I mean, I really am not interested.'

Lara adds, 'Neha, maybe it's time you looked for something that you actually enjoyed. I always assumed that you do like what you are doing since you never really complain, but now that you are not even willing to take on more, maybe you aren't happy.'

What is going on? I am happy. I do like my job. But I just don't like working. I know that is not an excuse, but still. Do I really want more responsibility?

'No, I am happy. I really like what I am doing, and my office and all that, but I just don't know if I am ready for all that extra responsibility.'

'How will you know if you don't take the chance?' challenges Lara.

'But why should I? I am so happy where I am.'

'Look, this new year, why don't you decide to take all the risks that you haven't before. Apply for the new position, work harder and make it work with Ishaan.'

I grumble while I sip on the remains of my drink.

'And maybe cut down on your drinks?' suggests Sanya playfully.

'Oh Neha, don't get cranky, we are just telling you this for your own good, and it's about time you started to grow up and take more responsibility,' Palak reaches over to hug me.

'Fine! I shall apply for the damn position.'

'And?' demands Lara.

'And make it work with Ishaan.'

'Good girl. Here they are now, so smile and go hug Ishaan,' instructs Lara.

I get up from my barstool with some difficulty and bound, grinning foolishly, towards Ishaan. Ishaan sees me and he almost picks me up in a hug. Two and a half tequila sunrises down and I don't quite care who is watching.

He smiles down at me, 'Quite tipsy, aren't we?'

I giggle in return. He smiles widely and kisses my forehead.

He cups my face pushing my hair away, 'I love you,' he smiles.

I gasp back in surprise. I didn't realize that this was coming so soon.

I give a foolish, love-struck smile. 'I love you too, Ishaan,' and I go on tiptoes to kiss him passionately right by the entrance.

Is this too much too soon? How did everything happen so quickly?

'Come on, let's go in, they're all staring at us!' he kisses my cheek. Holding hands we greet the others. While we chit chat in excited tones about Palak's engagement, I hear a husky woman's voice boom from the back.

'Hi, Ishaan.'

I turn around to a gorgeous dusky girl, Ishaan's date at Aer who had wanted to trample on me with her gigantic frame.

'Oh, hey,' Ishaan greets her.

I turn away immediately. My heart drops down to my stomach, my face turns red and I get this nauseated feeling.

It's unbearable to see Ishaan next to one of his exes or whatever they are called. I don't even want to hear their conversation. I knew it, it was too soon. And it was too good to be true. Once a player, always a player.

Ishaan's arm wraps around my waist and he pulls me back towards him.

'You remember Neha? Meet Neha, my girlfriend,' he smiles proudly.

I stand there, stunned, in front of the tall, striking woman. This is the first time I have been introduced like this.

And it feels good. Brilliant actually. Despite being towered over by a gorgeous Greek goddess.

'Hi,' I smile sweetly.

She looks me up and down, snorts and walks away.

'Wow! She definitely thinks you downgraded from beautiful to hideous with a weird nose!' I pout.

Ishaan holds me tighter, 'Shut up. Don't ever say that. You are beautiful and I am super happy being with you.'

I smile back, 'It felt good being introduced as your girlfriend.'

'It feels good to tell the world you are my girlfriend,' he kisses my head. 'I love you. Now I'm not letting you go anywhere tonight. You are staying right next to me in my arms throughout.'

I shiver excitedly as Ishaan tightens his grip around me.

YOU CANNOT ALWAYS TAKE THE RIGHT DECISION; HOWEVER YOU CAN TAKE A DECISION AND MAKE IT RIGHT

Today is 9 January 2012, the evening of Palak and Raj's engagement party.

The engagement party is exactly how Palak envisioned it. The lavender-and-gold scheme sparkles under the crystal chandeliers of the Regal Room. Although it's a small and intimate ceremony, the venue looks grand. A small stage is assembled at the end of the palatial ballroom and is decorated with lilies, orchids and other flowers with purple and white shades. The cream-coloured backdrop has designs matching the invitation card.

Palak and Raj greet the guests joyously. Palak looks radiant in her Tarun Tahiliani Swarovski diamond-studded lehenga. Raj matches her in a cream embroidered sherwani with a lilac-coloured dupatta. This evening is about Palak's dream coming true, a dream she had nurtured since childhood; and according to me, Raj is just a prop! She hadn't given that much thought the kind of guy she would be standing with as much as she had on the details of the ring, stage, flowers, colours and food!

Palak and Sanya have concocted a delicious vegetarian menu to satisfy every palate. Scrumptious appetizers of mini mushroom quiches, cocktail samosas, grilled tikkas and dips. The main course has both typical Gujarati food as well as an Asian fare of Burmese khao suey, pad Thai noodles, Thai curries and rice. The dessert bar is filled with all my favourite treats: mini cupcakes with lavender butter cream frosting, fortune cookies in purple-laced baskets, chocolate-dipped strawberries and grapes, little Chinese takeout boxes filled with chocolate chip cookies fastened with purple ribbons, marshmallow sticks, lavender-infused macaroons, mini éclairs and brownies with purple confetti. A round three-tiered cake covered in white fondant and a trail of delicate lavender sugar flowers are placed on a trolley with champagne bottles chilling in buckets of ice, ready to be wheeled onto the centrestage for the engaged couple.

Ishaan sneaks up on me from behind, 'Hi baby!' and he slides his arms around my bare waist showing above my turquoise lehenga.

I am startled as my body is conquered by a wave of goosebumps.

'Ishaan!' I exclaim worriedly, 'My parents are here! What's wrong with you?'

'So what? Your mum likes me. And shouldn't she be knowing that her daughter is finally in safe hands?'

'You're *safe* now? The city's biggest player is now safe?' I tease.

'Very, very safe because I know I have the world's most precious diamond in my hands and I will never let it drop,' he whispers in my ear and tickles my stomach.

I feel my face redden uncontrollably as I try to squirm out of his grasp.

'Stand still, your mum is looking at us,' he whispers.

'Yeah right, if she were, you'd have run away by now!' I laugh, gently elbowing his stomach.

'Neha,' my mother shrieks.

Oh shit!

My mother's voice jolts me out of my romantic mood. Ishaan stands still with his arms firmly wrapped around me, grinning mischievously while I try to twist away.

'Did you fall again? You are unbelievable, Neha. Ishaan, thank God for you, or else she would have created a scene here!' my mother exclaims loudly as she walks towards us, decked up in an elegant cream-coloured sari with an emerald green necklace, her hair tied up in a sophisticated French knot, showing off her large solitaires.

'Oh don't worry, Aunty, I will always be catching your daughter to safety,' Ishaan smiles like a fool.

'Thank you, Ishaan. Neha, come here, let me fix your dupatta.'

As she pushes one end here and re-pins another end, I stand flustered and dumbfounded. Ishaan looks on, beaming like an idiot and has the audacity to wink when I frown at him. Someone calls out 'Sheila' and she quickly walks away to greet other equally Botoxed ladies.

'How are you so calm?' I whisper.

'Why shouldn't I be? I am your boyfriend and I'd like your parents to know that,' Ishaan replies.

Oh shit. Do I really want to bring this up at an engagement? That too, at Palak's? No, Neha. No drama here.

'Why won't you tell your parents about us?' Ishaan asks with serious concern.

'Because my mother will go bonkers and get us married by next week. I don't think you want that!'

'Well, I would want to at some point. Wouldn't you?' I stare at him stunned.

Of course I do. I want to marry him right now and have all his babies. But at the same time . . . I really don't know. Palak's engagement places a face to my mystery man; it's Ishaan and only Ishaan. How is it possible that he has been right in front of me for all these years yet I never saw him in my dreams? Or never realized that he is the one? Wouldn't I have known?

'Shhh . . . Ishaan, later. Not here.'

'Are you brushing me off?' he asks, clearly offended.

'No. I just want to take it step by step. You know, what if you change your mind? We barely know each other.'

'We've been friends for the past five years, about the same time since Palak and Raj started dating,' he responds quietly. 'No, Neha, I will only say things I mean. I don't say stuff just for the heck of it.'

'Ishaan, let's just talk about this later. The ceremony is going to begin.' I quickly run away to find Sanya and Lara, feeling even more jittery than being caught by my mother.

Shit. Lifelong commitment. With Ishaan? Can I trust him? Yeah, right! Falling for Ishaan, although it feels amazing, can also turn into the biggest heartbreak in the history of heartbreaks. Is it worth taking the plunge? Arrghhh! Why won't someone just tell me what to do? So I know if I should go that extra mile. Or two. Shit, should I be holding back? Just because I am scared? Oh God, show me some sign at least!

The guests crowd around the stage to watch Palak and Raj sitting on their lilac-ribboned thrones, flanked by their families. Palak's mother looks on as Palak and Raj exchange a joke and chuckle, holding hands. The past few months had been a crazy journey for them and Palak's mother is still in a bewildered state, wondering about what happened. Palak glows in her finery and Raj never looked happier. Sanya, Lara and I stand close by, admiring their fairytale moment.

'She really was stupid to almost throw that outfit out. I would've taken it too!' comments Sanya.

'Yeah I know, it's just gorgeous.'

'Don't forget the official story of Raj's proposal,' warns Lara.

Sanya and I exchange evil grins.

'Oh yes, of course, we remember,' I snigger.

Raj had given us strict instructions not to spill the beans about his actual proposal. He wasn't too comfortable about flaunting his romantic side and the minor detail of them having a pre-wedding honeymoon in a hotel room in Goa! Palak couldn't care less, but Raj is slightly more conservative and worried about the parents' reactions.

'Are you having second thoughts?' whispers Ishaan from behind.

Dammit! How the hell does he always creep up on me like that?

'Ishaan! No, I am not!' I whisper back.

Sanya and Lara stare at us, wondering what is going on. I shake my head to drive off any ideas they might be forming about us.

Raj slips the three-carat ring on Palak's finger once again while everyone cheers. After the loud round of applause, Palak and Raj climb down the steps of the stage and we rush to hug and kiss them.

'Thank you!' Palak squeals. 'Now you're next, Neha!' she winks mischievously before moving on to thank other well-wishers. I freeze, aware that Ishaan is standing right behind and must have heard every word Palak just yelled. I quickly walk away red-faced, jumpy and nervous, only to be called back for the cake cutting.

Maybe some cake will make me feel better.

As Palak and Raj cut the cake, Ishaan and Ashish pop open the champagne bottles for the couple. Despite being so tempted by the cake, I can't take my eyes off Ishaan. He secretly smiles at me as he pops open a bottle and pours out two glasses. Everyone toasts to the health, wealth and prosperous future for the couple before guzzling down some bubbly. A live band sings *At Last*, Palak's song, in the background.

Sanya is chatting and giggling away with Vick and Abhi. She looks happy. Content. Sanjay seems to be the last thing on her mind. She had kept herself busy with Palak's engagement and helped her turn her dream into a reality. But now that this is over, what next? Planning for Lara's wedding?

The free-flowing champagne and red strawberries (Palak would have liked them to be purple!) keep us in high spirits throughout the evening. The luscious, moist and dark chocolate sponge cake with thin layers of vanilla and pistachio butter cream frosting also help. The lavender fondant flowers are gorgeous little treats.

But even this bit of heavenly goodness cannot keep my mind off Ishaan and our relationship.

I grab Lara by the arm.

'How do you know whether it is or not?'

'What?' she asks confused.

'I mean how do you know when to make that extra effort? What sign did you get when you knew you wanted to marry Ashish and so you made all these sacrifices and compromises and all that other love shit?'

'Oh my God, Neha! Are you serious? You're waiting for a sign? No one is going to come and tell you whether or not you are with the right person. If you love that person, you go that extra mile. You push yourself to make it work, work and work until it does. Geez Neha, if you sat around and waited for a sign each time you'd be single forev—. . .' she stops abruptly and stares at me with her eyes wide open. 'Ohhh . . . no wonder, Neha! No! You cannot run away from Ishaan. He's just too good to be true . . . and so dreamy,' her eyes turn lovestruck.

'Okay, I get it Lara, stop drooling!' I snap back, agitated.

'Neha, I'm being serious, you cannot run or escape this time. Face whatever you have to. There are no promises. Just trials and errors. We have to make our own decisions and that's how we create our own destiny.'

'Can you make the decision for me?' I ask lamely.

'Yes, I will. You are to be with Ishaan, no matter what it takes,' she orders strictly.

'Yes, ma'am,' I smile gratefully.

Another order to follow; one that I really like. I turn around and look for Ishaan.

'Neha, don't screw it up,' Lara warns threateningly as I walk away.

I find Ishaan in conversation with Sanya and . . . *oh shit, my mother.*

Sanya darts me an evil grin. I rush over, fearfully aware that Sanya is capable of doing everything stupid and humiliating.

'Neha!' Sanya calls out, sashaying in her sari with its light pink and orange pallu. 'So you haven't told your mother about your boyfriend then?'

Shit. I knew it. That bitch just loves to see me squirm.

'Sanya, shut up!' I seethe with rage.

'What boyfriend?' my mother asks immediately.

'Uh, nothing Mum, Sanya is talking nonsense as usual.'

Ishaan starts to shift uncomfortably.

'Neha?' he asks quietly.

'Umm . . .' I mumble while my mum's eyes pierce right through mine.

'Actually, Mum, I do have a boyfriend,' I take the leap.

'Who?' Her voice shrill with worry.

'Umm . . .'

'Umm . . . it's me, Aunty,' Ishaan places his hand on the small of my back comfortingly.

My mother stares in shock at him and then at me for a whole minute. We wait anxiously for a reaction.

Then she bursts out laughing, 'Oh come on, that's a good joke! You and my daughter, Ishaan? However much I wish it would happen, I know I'm keeping my hopes too high!' She shakes her head as she pulls his cheek affectionately and walks off laughing.

We stare after her in disbelief!

'What the hell does she mean? That I'm not good enough for you?' My eyes are on the verge of tears.

'Eh, come on, she is just joking around,' Sanya comforts me by putting her arms around me. 'I am so sorry, I would never have brought it up if I knew this would have happened.'

'No, it's okay. It's actually kind of funny that I said the truth and she didn't believe me! At least now she can never say that I was trying to hide anything. But see, everyone, including my own mother, thinks we make an odd couple!'

'Oh shut up, Neha. No one thinks that. I love you and I only want to be with you.'

'Go away, you . . . you . . . giant tree!' I say gently, punching him in his stomach.

Sanya and Ishaan burst out laughing and Ishaan bends down to kiss my cheek.

'Come on, let's get you a cupcake,' he laughs. 'See that brought back your beautiful smile! Sanya, does her face light up just as much at the mention of my name?'

Sanya responds cheekily, 'Not as much as the mention of candy, but close enough!'

As the last of the guests trickle out, Lara, Ashish, Sanya, Vick, Abhi, Ishaan and I seat ourselves down to have dinner with Raj and Palak. At the round table, Sanya makes a shocking announcement.

'I have news for you, guys,' she says.

'Uh oh . . . is it bad?' I ask, concerned.

'No, actually,' she smiles calmly. 'It's really good,' exchanging glances with Palak.

'What does Palak know that we don't?' demands Lara.

'I am moving to New York!' Sanya smiles widely.

'What?' I blurt out horrified. 'Why? You can't leave us!' I insist.

'But why?' asks a confused Lara.

'I applied for a course at NYU. It's a sixteen-month course in social work. It starts this spring. So, I have to leave soon!'

'That's great news!'

'No, it is the worst news ever!' I cry out. 'You cannot go!'

'Neha, I need to get out of here. I can't be in this city much longer. I need to go to a new place, meet new people and gain a new perspective. And I think I need to find a new purpose in life,' she looks at me. 'Being a social bird and doing nothing hasn't really helped me. It's time I do something a little more productive. I really do need to get out of here for a while.'

Palak adds, 'I helped her out with the applications and the rest of the stuff. I think she is making a wise decision, she has to do something more with her life. I think she should be moving forward and venturing towards new horizons.'

'Shit, what the hell are we going to do without you?'

'Neha, did you apply for the position?' asks Lara sternly.

'Yes, I did apply. Although I found out that Tanya is also applying so I am sure I don't have much of a chance,' I shrug.

'What? That is great news, baby!' says Ishaan, supporting me. 'Why didn't you say anything?'

'It doesn't matter if you get it or not; you applied and made that effort and that means something.'

'I think we should toast to that—to new beginnings!' Abhi declares.

I smile as I sip on my champagne.

New beginnings indeed.

'Dude, I just feel really old all of a sudden!' says Vick sombrely.

We burst out laughing.

'Yeah, we are getting old and responsible! Including Sanya and Neha!' comments Lara cheekily.

'To new beginnings!' smiles Sanya.

FOOTPRINTS

A JOURNEY OF A THOUSAND MILES MUST BEGIN WITH A SINGLE STEP

The new year brought in many new beginnings.

I did not get the promotion at work, Tanya did; and I now work under her. I'm not heartbroken with this turn of events, as I know I didn't work hard enough. I had already figured I didn't have a chance once Tanya entered the race. Actually, I never had a chance at it, period. But working under Tanya has now given me a sense of drive to achieve more and entering my fourth year at the same level of work is beginning to prickle me. It's gradually dawning on me that I am no longer content at doing just this. That I even tried for the promotion is a start to my new perspective on life.

I finally sat my parents down and told them about Ishaan. It took my mother quite some convincing to finally believe me. She was sure that I was being delusional or was just messing with her head. Once she digested the fact that her daughter is actually seriously dating a handsome and dashing young man, she went ballistic (in a good way) and now Ishaan gets all the importance in my house. I don't mind since we are very happy in love. I wake up every morning with a smile on my face, I notice the birds chirping, I revel in the traffic jams that allow me to chat at leisure with Ishaan, and we never tire of each other. We have already started talking about our future and spend hours planning hypothetical situations. I'm secretly pining for a destination wedding in Goa, the place where we unexpectedly fell in love with each other. But, a proposal still awaits . . .

Sanya left for New York, promising to be in touch and more importantly, to be good. We all know how long that is going to last! She has managed to kick Sanjay completely out of her life and her steely determination to succeed has returned. News is that Sanya has already embraced the streets of Manhattan.

Lara has started working on the interiors of her new home as well as planning her wedding for this year. She still isn't on talking terms with her mother-in-law, but Divya and Riya occasionally meet her for coffee. Lara's love is gradually winning over her in-laws, much to Ashish's relief and Lara's satisfaction.

Palak is now working with Raj in his solo venture. She has decided that she wants to help Raj first establish himself and then focus on her own career. They make a perfect team and plan to get married next year.

Harry and Monica continue to be our clients at work; they create havoc at every meeting. Monica, the adulterous bitch, still makes me jittery while Harry darling and Rita continue their love affair in her private chambers.

Some things don't change . . .

ACKNOWLEDGEMENTS

I could never have achieved such a big feat without the support of many special ones.

A hearty thank you goes out to my family. Mummy, for being a beautiful mother, my best friend and for supporting me throughout this crazy adventure. Pappa, for passing on your sense of humour, showing me the lighter side of every catastrophe and proving there is a method in the madness. Naman, for being a sensible guide, anchor and big brother, always. My rather large, boisterous and eccentric extended family: nana, mama, mami, masa, masis and cousins, without whom life would be forever dull in my new home. Thank you for being yourselves and thereby being a source of unending fun—special thanks to Meenamasi and Ilamasi!

Nitya Somany Patel, thank you very much for reading patiently through every draft; your creative input has been instrumental in shaping what *The Morning After* is today. A big shout out to my friends Prachi, Purnimaa, Urvi, Nisha, Karishma, Shreya, Sajni and Amrita for being a source of energy, happiness and laughter and encouraging me to continue doing wonderful things in my life, no matter how crazy! And, of course, thank you everyone who has been and is a part of my life and made me who I am today (you know who you are!).

Most importantly, my greatest gratitude is for Vaishali Mathur, senior commissioning editor at Penguin Books India, for offering me this unbelievable opportunity and for being a stellar guide and confidante throughout the publishing process. And last, but not least, thank you Paloma Dutta, copy editor at Penguin, for sorting out the nitty-gritties, allowing me to keep the cuss words and ensuring a great final manuscript!